"It sounds like you have a nice little business."

"I like making the dolls." Eliza smoothed down a tiny dress, and her voice grew animated. "The money I bring in helps with the household income, too. Levy and Jane have been so *gut* to me, so I'm glad to be helping out."

"Your eyes are sparkling," he observed. A smile played across his face.

She jerked her head up and immediately blanked her expression. Was he flirting? Whatever hidden hurt feelings she carried—or, for that matter, he harbored—she would not allow them to come to the surface. "We were talking about the dolls," she reminded him.

"*Ja*, sure. The dolls." He looked down at the box of toys. "But I understand your enthusiasm. I admire how you're taking your worldly experience and using it to the good. It's like you're countering the bad examples you witnessed. There's something to be said for that, Eliza."

"*Danke.*" She felt wary of his praise. He was not meant for her…

Living on a remote self-sufficient homestead in North Idaho, **Patrice Lewis** is a Christian wife, mother, author, blogger, columnist and speaker. She has practiced and written about rural subjects for almost thirty years. When she isn't writing, Patrice enjoys self-sufficiency projects, such as animal husbandry, small-scale dairy production, gardening, food preservation and canning, and homeschooling. She and her husband have been married since 1990 and have two daughters.

Books by Patrice Lewis

Love Inspired

Visit the Author Profile page at Harlequin.com.

Her Path to
Redemption

Patrice Lewis

LOVE INSPIRED
INSPIRATIONAL ROMANCE

LOVE INSPIRED®
INSPIRATIONAL ROMANCE

Recycling programs
for this product may
not exist in your area.

ISBN-13: 978-1-335-56713-0

Her Path to Redemption

Copyright © 2021 by Patrice Lewis

This edition published by arrangement with Harlequin Books S.A.

For questions and comments about the quality of this book, please contact us at CustomerService@Harlequin.com.

Love Inspired
22 Adelaide St. West, 40th Floor
Toronto, Ontario M5H 4E3, Canada
www.Harlequin.com

Printed in U.S.A.

Keep thy tongue from evil,
and thy lips from speaking guile.
—*Psalm* 34:13

To God, for blessing me with my husband and daughters, the best family anyone could hope for.

Chapter One

Through the open kitchen window, Eliza Struder felt the soft breeze that ruffled the maple leaves off the back porch. Early morning sun dappled the side of the small white farmhouse, and a veritable chorus of birdsong poured through the window. Nearby, the garden gleamed in the morning light. The glossy, tender leaves of young corn whispered in the background, and the abundant strawberry leaves hid their ruby treasures.

Eliza stared out at the verdant landscape, lost in thought. A year ago she had been staring out a different kitchen window in a dingy little apartment in Seattle, newly widowed and heavily pregnant, wondering why she had ever thought it necessary to leave her secure Amish roots and explore the exciting *Englisch* world that had turned out not to be so exciting after all.

Now she was home, living with her brother and sister-in-law, raising her baby daughter, Mercy…but her future was no less uncertain.

She turned and peered into the small mirror near the kitchen door and concentrated on subduing her hair under her starched *kapp* as the family got ready to attend a barn expansion project for a neighbor.

After the third time she dropped the hairpins meant to secure the head covering, her sister-in-law, Jane, glanced over. "You're nervous," she observed.

"*Ja*, maybe." Eliza jammed in another pin. "I know I shouldn't be, but I am."

"Is it because Josiah will be there?"

"Maybe."

"I'll take that as a *ja*." Jane raised an eyebrow. "You've been home nine months now. Does he still rattle you?" Jane held back little Mercy. "No, *liebling*, your *mamm* is busy right now."

"That's all right, I'm finished." Eliza bent to scoop the year-old child into her arms. She nuzzled the baby's neck, then looked over at Jane. "Yes, Josiah rattles me. But I'm not the right woman for him, and that's that."

"Don't be so sure." Jane finished securing her own *kapp* and gave herself an indifferent glance in the mirror. "I've seen him watching you. He still isn't married for a reason."

"Jane, don't tease." The words came out sharper than she intended. Eliza shook her head. "I'm sorry. I'm taking my nerves out on you. That's not fair."

"As I recall, I felt the same way about your brother before I married him." Jane adjusted her apron. "He rattled me all the time. I just didn't know he felt the same way. I'm not pretty—not like you are—and I never hoped he could look past that and love me back."

On impulse, Eliza leaned over and kissed Jane on the cheek. "I'm the most blessed of women to have you as a sister. I'm so glad Levy married you."

Jane's eyes grew soft behind her glasses. *"Ja,"* she said. *"Gott* never fails us, does He? Levy is the best thing to ever happen to me."

Eliza felt a moment of envy at her sister-in-law's transparent happiness. She sometimes wondered what *Gott* had up His sleeve for her own future.

But it wasn't likely to involve Josiah Lapp, the stable, handsome boy she'd thrown over when the lures of the wider world overcame her. In the excitement of exploring the beautiful city of Seattle, staying with an *Englisch* girlfriend who had given her a couch to sleep on, in the novelty of wearing stylish non-Amish clothing she selected in thrift stores, in the fun of working a retail job and earning her own money—she'd forgotten about Josiah. Instead she'd married a wild, exciting *Englischer*, a marriage she regretted within weeks.

Josiah didn't enter her thoughts again until, in her widowed state, her daughter, Mercy, was born and Eliza had sent her precious infant to be raised by her brother. Then she wondered what Josiah was doing and whom he had married. She wondered what he thought of her.

Now that she was home, she still didn't know his thoughts.

But for now, she was sure what she needed to do. She needed to take care of Mercy. She needed to make a contribution to her brother's household, since she was living under his roof. She needed to decide whether or not she wanted to be baptized. And she needed—above all—to avoid Josiah Lapp, the man who once loved her.

It wasn't only that he tempted her to want something—someone—she couldn't have. She knew she was closely watched in the community to see if she had truly embraced its values again upon her return. She couldn't afford to stumble when she was so close to achieving her goal of full immersion in the faith of her family.

Jane finished packing a basket with cold fried chicken and macaroni salad. "Why so pensive today?"

"I don't know." Eliza bounced Mercy gently. "I have no regrets becoming a mother, but I wish I'd gone about it differently. You know— less wild, more wisdom." She never, ever dared voice the secret wish that her baby's father had been Josiah. "I'm grateful you and Levy were able to care for Mercy when I couldn't. And I'm grateful you took me back in when I needed it. It's given me a chance to get back on my feet."

"That's what family is for." Jane hefted the basket into her arms. "*Komm.* I think Levy has the horse hitched up to the buggy now. We don't want to be late."

Josiah Lapp helped his mother, Ruby, into the wagon seat, then lifted a basket of food into her lap. "Let me get my things loaded and I'll be ready to go."

He hefted a tool belt and box into the back of the wagon, then climbed into the seat beside his mother and picked up the reins. "Let's go, boys!" The horses started off with a small jolt.

He was silent, thinking about the barn expansion project he was heading toward. Doubtless Eliza would be there, since her brother, Levy, was helping with the project. Most people he knew would be there, in fact. But Eliza was the one he dreaded seeing.

His mother interrupted his thoughts. "It's a

nice day for the barn expansion. But I hope you won't be so busy that you can't eat lunch with Jodie."

With difficulty, Josiah forced his mind away from Eliza. "Who's Jodie?"

"Don't you remember? She's the young woman you met last Sabbath."

Josiah vaguely remembered the pretty blonde who hovered around him, the latest of his mother's attempts to shove an eligible woman in his path. He sighed. "*Mamm*, I wish you wouldn't do this."

"Do what?" Ruby's voice was guileless.

"Try to involve me with various women."

"Someone has to. You always say you're too busy to court anyone."

"I'm just not ready to get married yet."

"Why not? You're in a nice position. Your business is doing well. You could easily support a family."

"*Ja*, but… But I'm just not ready."

"I hope you're not still hung up on Eliza Struder." His mother's voice was sharp.

"*Nein*. I'm just not ready to get married."

"*Gut*, because she's not the right woman for you."

Josiah suppressed the resentment he always felt at his mother's interference in his personal life. His mother had taken widowhood hard, and Josiah tried to be patient with her even as he mourned his father's passing.

But Ruby had shown uncharacteristic hostility toward Eliza ever since that prodigal daughter had returned to the community. Josiah was twisted up in knots about his feelings for Eliza. He didn't need his mother's constant harping about why Eliza was an unsuitable match for him.

"I'll be the judge of that," he answered noncommittally, then changed the subject. "What did you pack in the hamper for lunch? I hope you included my favorite pie."

"Blueberry." Distracted, Ruby touched the lid of the hamper. "*Ja*, a full blueberry pie, just for you."

"*Danke*. I'll try not to eat the whole thing by myself."

They lapsed into silence again as the horse pulled the wagon toward the home where the barn expansion was taking place.

And there she was. Among the brightly dressed women, he picked Eliza out immediately in a forest-green dress and black apron. She carried Mercy on one hip while holding a basket, walking with her sister-in-law, Jane, toward a series of tables set out in the shade of some maples in the farmhouse's yard. Her dark blond hair was tucked neatly under her *kapp* and he could see the gleam of humor in her eyes as she said something to Jane.

He jerked his gaze away and directed his wagon around to the parking area, assisted his mother down, unhitched the horses and prepared to spend the day working with the other men. It would be easy to avoid Eliza. Easy as… as blueberry pie.

As he started off to work, he thought of his future. His mother was right. His construction business was doing well. He could easily support a family. The community was full of eligible young women. Why couldn't he just pick one?

Deep down, he knew the answer. Next to the fiery Eliza, every other young woman seemed tame and bland.

For now, he wouldn't focus on her. Instead, he needed to support his widowed mother, to expand his construction business…and maybe find someone to settle down with.

Eliza was not the right woman for him. He wanted a wife, *ja*, but she should not have a wild streak in her. He needed to find someone sedate and mature, someone uncontaminated by the lures of the wider world…a world he had learned to distrust after Eliza left.

Gott had taught him a hard lesson through Eliza's departure. He needed to find a wife more

suitable than the rebellious girl he'd once loved, someone who would not drag down his standing in the community. He couldn't ignore *Gott*'s hand in this. He had to make the right choice.

He would leave the details up to *Gott*.

With a basket of rolls in her hands, Eliza rounded a corner of the house and bumped square into the last man she wanted to see. The impact made her stagger and it knocked Josiah's straw hat off his head. She clutched the basket lest she spill the rolls. "Excuse me."

Reflexively Josiah steadied her, then dropped his hands and shoved them into his pockets, as if touching her repulsed him. "Sorry," he muttered.

Eliza stood very still, trying not to betray her emotions. His dark blue eyes were unsmiling and wary. Josiah had matured in the years she was out in the *Englisch* world. He wasn't a tall man, but he was solid and muscular, with curly brown hair that gave him a boyish look despite his unsmiling expression. His tool belt added to his manly appearance.

"I'm clumsy…" she began.

"As long as I didn't hurt you," he said.

Eliza nearly winced at the double meaning of the term. She was the one who had hurt him, not the other way around. She'd hurt him by tossing his youthful courtship in his face and leaving the community. Her throat grew tight.

"Josiah… Can we still be friends?" she choked. "I've been home since last fall, and you've hardly said two words to me."

"What do you want me to say?" he replied, a note of weariness in his voice. "You've changed. I've changed. Nothing can ever be the same."

"Say you've forgiven me."

His expression became hooded. "It would be uncharitable of me not to say I've forgiven you. But you must admit, Eliza, you've made some bad decisions in your life. I'm just grateful I wasn't part of them."

Josiah spun on his heel, snatched his hat off the ground and marched off. She saw the rigid set of his shoulders beneath the white shirt as he plunked his hat back on his head.

Tears prickled her eyes. Okay, Josiah hated her. That was obvious. She knew she had hurt him deeply when she left the community during her *rumspringa*, and now her chickens were coming home to roost. Some fallout from her actions was expected.

Except… It hurt.

As much as she wanted to call after him, to ask for a chance to explain, she stifled that urge. Her temper and her impulsiveness had led her astray in the past when she'd been angry about

everything, even angry at *Gott* for taking her
parents away. She needed to learn obedience
and acceptance. She bit the inside of her mouth
and watched as he walked over to a pretty young
woman she knew was called Jodie, who smiled
at him. Eliza watched as Josiah's posture relaxed, and he smiled back.

Eliza still felt the brief grip of Josiah's hands
on her upper arms when he'd steadied her after
their collision. She also remembered how fast
he'd yanked his hands away and buried them
in his pockets, as if disgusted by the physical
contact.

What if? What if she'd never left her hometown? What if the last few years had been spent
in courtship and marriage with Josiah? What if
Mercy had been his? What if?

She'd seen enough. Clutching the basket of
rolls, she turned to find an empty spot on a
loaded table. But she felt a jolt as she intercepted
a look from Ruby Lapp.

Josiah's widowed mother didn't like her. The
older woman was vocal in her objections to the
idea of Eliza's baptism. Since baptism required
unanimous community consent, Ruby's attitude
was a formidable barrier. Feminine instinct told
her the older woman's attitude stemmed from
how Eliza had treated her son before disappear-
ing among the *Englisch*.

As she turned away from the tables she was helping fill with food, Eliza sighed. Life was never simple, and Eliza knew she had only herself to blame for Ruby's attitude. Josiah had wanted to court her several years before, when they were both in their late teens. But she had been restless and rebellious, determined to leave behind the stability of her church roots, spread her wings and see the world.

So she left. Left her town of Grand Creek, Indiana, left the Amish and embraced the *Englisch* culture. What happened next was worse than anything she could have envisioned.

Seeing her daughter toddling under the watchful eye of her sister-in-law, Eliza went over to scoop up the baby. She hugged the child close. Mercy was the only good thing to come out of those tumultuous years.

She was home now, and had promised *Gott* to be a better woman in the future than she had been in the past. But Ruby disliked her, she knew, because Josiah never married after Eliza had left him in the lurch.

Eliza sighed again. She had made enough mistakes in her life. She didn't have to make more by throwing her heart where it wasn't wanted, especially if her behavior drew negative attention when she was trying to live a pure and Godly life. She would leave Josiah strictly alone to court whatever woman he could find and lead a happy, stable life.

But the lump in her chest proved she was experiencing regret. Deep, bitter regret.

From across the lawn, Josiah sat with a plate of tasteless food in front of him and tried to be pleasant to Jodie, the latest of his mother's matchmaking selections.

Covertly, he watched Eliza as she alternated between setting up the meal and attending to the needs of her baby. A lump settled in his chest, and he finally recognized it for what it was: regret. Even grief. It was too late for them. There would never be a courtship between them. She had too much baggage—nor was she baptized—and he was too angry with her for what she'd done.

He wondered if Eliza had any idea the anguish he'd suffered after she left the community. He'd loved her then, despite her wild streak, and he thought she loved him back. Apparently he was wrong.

She was different now. Older. Not just in years, but in experience. She was no longer the vivacious teen, but a grown woman—wife, widow and mother in fast succession. Her dark blond hair was damp from the day's humidity, but properly pinned up and tucked beneath her *kapp*. Her dark blue eyes were serious as she spoke to her brother and sister-in-law. She'd been, as the *Englisch* like to say, through the School of Hard Knocks.

What if? What if Eliza had never left? What if the last few years had been spent in their own courtship and marriage? What if the baby she held in her arms was his, not some wild *Englischer*'s who had married Eliza and then died in a car crash? What if?

He'd spent the last few years coming to terms with uncharacteristic fury at her. Such deep-seated anger was discouraged within the church, and he was ashamed he felt such an emotion, but it couldn't be helped. It was too late for them. There would never be a courtship between them.

His mother, knowing his pain, shared his resentment toward Eliza, as well. Yes, this prodigal daughter was someone devoutly to be avoided.

Josiah understood he was going against *Gott*'s will by harboring a secret hope he could ever marry Eliza. He was also keenly aware of how many eyes were watching her, weighing her behavior, judging her actions. He didn't want to do anything that might jeopardize her path to redemption.

He was, he realized, still seething with deep, bitter regret.

Sitting on a bench under an oak tree, Eliza picked up her daughter and snuggled the child against her shoulder. "I think she's getting tired." She reached into a basket and withdrew a doll. "There, *liebling*, here's your doll…"

"That's nice." Jane touched the traditional faceless Amish figure. "Did you make this?"

"*Ja*. I finished it this week."

"May I see it?"

Eliza gently pried the toy from her daughter's clutch and handed it to her sister-in-law, who examined it with an air of authority before handing it back. "I think you might consider making more of these. I'll bet they'd sell at the market."

Jane and Levy ran a booth at a Saturday farmers market, which kept them very busy during the summer. While Levy focused on farm produce to sell, Jane made jams, chutneys, salsas and baked goods to help stock the booth.

"Well, I've been trying to think of something I can contribute," mused Eliza. "Maybe I should consider it."

"You seem very determined to earn your own money," observed Jane gently. "But you're already helping make things for the market. Your strawberry preserves sold out last week, remember? And you're raising Mercy, as well."

"You did that, and more, last summer before I came home," replied Eliza. "You were Mercy's nanny at the same time you were helping Levy build up his farmers market business."

Jane smiled and shoved her glasses up her nose. "I'm just glad I didn't have to go away and never see her again." Jane laughed. "When I was her nanny, I fell in love with this *boppli*. Thankfully Levy wouldn't let me go after you came home. When I think how he chased me down in the buggy before I could get to the train station…"

"He's still crazy about you." Eliza didn't mean for a tone of pathos to creep in, but it did.

Jane's gaze sharpened and, with the emotional instinct Eliza had come to admire, pinpointed the misery behind her words. "It's Josiah, isn't it?"

"No." The word came out too fast, and she knew it. She sighed. "*Ja*, it's Josiah. It's sinful of me to still think about him."

"Do you know the girl he sat with at lunch?"

"I used to know her vaguely. Her name is Jodie. She's very nice. More importantly, she doesn't have a past like I do. Josiah would be a fool to give up someone like her, and he'd be a bigger fool to look at someone like me."

"How serious were you and Josiah before you left for the *Englisch* world?"

"It's hard to say." Eliza stroked her daughter's back. "We were too young to court, you understand. But we were friends, and friendship often turns into something more. Then I left."

"But then you came back."

"*Ja*, but Josiah didn't know I was going to come back. And why would he be interested in a woman as tainted as I am?"

"Is that what you think you are?" Jane's eyes widened. "Tainted?"

"*Ja*, of course."

"But Mercy wasn't born out of wedlock. You were married."

"*Ja*, but it was a marriage I regretted almost the moment it happened. And then when Bill was killed in a car accident, I felt horribly guilty that I wasn't sorry he was gone. I still feel guilty for that reason. It was a relief, not a tragedy. I wouldn't have been able to stay with him. I'm glad Mercy won't have him as a father." She was relieved to admit this without facing harsh judgment. It had bothered her at first that her grief had been so short and shallow. It had made her wonder if she was coldhearted.

"*Ja*, I can see how complicated you may feel.

But *Gott* forgives, Eliza. If you've prayed for forgiveness, *Gott* has given it. But now you have to forgive yourself."

"And that's what I haven't done yet." Eliza kept her eyes on her daughter. "And that's also why I don't want to encourage anything with Josiah. He needs to find a good woman. If he married Jodie, that would be a blessing."

"*Ja*, a blessing." Jane's voice was bland.

Eliza glanced at her. "You don't approve of Jodie?"

"I didn't say that. I hardly know her." Jane nodded across the lawn of visiting church members. "But I know someone who does, someone who approves of her highly."

"Who?"

"Ruby. Josiah's mother."

Eliza followed her sister-in-law's gaze toward the older woman. "*Ja*, I got that impression."

"It's more than an impression. I may be indulging in the sin of gossip, but I've heard it said Ruby is pushing her son to court Jodie because…" Her voice trailed off.

"Because she's not me."

"*Ja*. I think she's afraid Josiah may rekindle his interest in you, and Ruby doesn't want that."

"Ruby shouldn't be worried. I don't intend to cause any trouble between them. My future is in *Gott*'s hands now, and it's not my place to interrupt a courtship or create any conflict."

Jane smiled. "You *have* grown up."

"I had no choice." Eliza looked over toward the men. "I think Levy is ready to leave." She stood up and snuggled Mercy's head down on her shoulder. "But whatever *Gott* has in store for me, one thing is certain sure. I'm glad to be home. These are my people."

Josiah bid his fellow carpenters goodbye, then climbed into the wagon seat beside his mother. He took one last look at the expansion to the barn, now roofed and sided and ready for livestock. He gave a nod of satisfaction. "A job well done," he remarked. "That should last for generations."

Ruby sighed as the horses started down the road. "*Ach*, I'm tired. I'm not used to being on my feet so much anymore."

"I'm glad you're getting out more," Josiah told her. "You were staying home too much since *Daed* died."

"It was hard to face everyone without him." She patted his hand. "You're a *gut* son to take care of me. But *ja*, I know I should be getting out more." She paused for a moment, then added, "I saw you talking with Eliza Struder."

"I couldn't help but talk to her. We collided.

But don't worry, *Mamm*, I made it clear I was glad I wasn't involved in the bad decisions she's made in her life so far."

"Gut." Ruby's voice sounded relieved. "Because she *has* made bad decisions."

"Though some might say she's trying to redeem herself."

"Redemption can be a long and difficult road." Ruby's voice was bitter. "You don't need her kind of trouble in your life. She has a lot to prove."

Josiah glanced sharply at his mother, who bit her lip and kept her gaze on the passing landscape. There seemed more to that remark than met the eye. "What do you mean?"

"Nothing. Oh, look, the Miller's cow finally had her calf."

The obvious change of subject raised Josiah's eyebrows, but he didn't pursue the conversation further.

It wasn't his business to pry into his mother's private thoughts. He had enough on his plate as it was, and he took her warnings seriously about Eliza's troubles not becoming his. He'd seen some of the squinted looks aimed his way by friends and acquaintances when he'd spoken with Eliza earlier, and he suspected they were not filled with charitable thoughts. For her sake as well as his, he had to be careful.

Chapter Two

The morning sun shone bright through the kitchen windows, highlighting the sage and cream paint on the woodwork, the plain table and chairs, the cookstove that occupied a corner.

While Eliza fed Mercy applesauce, Jane bustled about setting the table for breakfast. The toddler's face, coated with puréed fruit, broke into a smile for her uncle when Levy entered the kitchen with two foaming pails of milk. *"Onkle!"*

"Liebling." Levy put the buckets on the counter and dropped a kiss on his niece's head.

"Breakfast is ready," Jane told her husband. "Come and eat."

After the silent blessing over the food, Eliza caught a glance between Jane and Levy. He nodded at his wife.

Jane looked over at Eliza and smiled. "We

thought you should know. I'm expecting our first baby."

Eliza froze in the process of lifting the applesauce spoon. A slow grin spread across her face. "Congratulations! That's wonderful!"

"Ja." Jane hugged herself and raised her eyes upward. "I'm so happy!"

"You always said your gift from *Gott* is soothing babies. Now you get to have your own. Oh, Jane, I'm glad."

"Me, too." Levy speared a piece of bacon, a broad smile on his face. "But it does mean the house is going to become a bit small, especially since we hope *Gott* sends us lots of *bopplis.*" He bit into the bacon and spoke after swallowing. "I've been going over our finances, and I think we can swing some carpenters to build an addition. Better to do it now, before more children come and our money might be tighter."

"Ja, I can understand that. *Daed* and *Mamm* never had a reason to make the *haus* bigger, since it was just the two of us." Eliza looked around the kitchen. "It's also too small to ever host a Sabbath service. What are you thinking of doing?"

"Building outward, off the living room." Levy gestured. "An addition over there would allow a second floor to be joined with our current second floor. It would be a big project, and will be fairly disruptive for most of the summer, but I'll have to hire a crew to do it since I'm too busy with the farmers market to handle the work myself."

"It's a busy time of year for the carpentry crews," observed Eliza. "You'll have to see who's available."

"*Ja*, that could be a problem." Levy ran a hand over his beard, glanced at his wife, and raised an eyebrow with meaning. "I'll start making inquiries."

Josiah thinned his mouth. "*Ja*, we're available. But Levy, surely you know this might be awkward…"

"I thought of that." Levy spread the rough drawing of his vision for the house expansion on the desk. "But your crew is *gut*, and your prices are right. It's not like you'll even have to see Eliza."

"Of course I'll see her. She lives there, doesn't she?"

"*Ja*, but you'll be working outside, and she'll be taking care of the baby. Or helping Jane."

Josiah shook his head. "I don't know, Levy…"

"There's no one else available."

Josiah knew that was true. All the Amish carpenter crews worked hard throughout the sum-

mer while the weather was good. He had just
finished a project on another house.

"Besides," continued Levy, "didn't you once
tell me you sometimes bypass other jobs because you prefer to keep your crew working
only within the Plain community?"

"*Ja*, but…"

"Well, here's a job for you. And a big one,
too," concluded Levy.

Josiah knew the reason for his reluctance to
work on *Englischer* projects. The woman he'd
loved had been lured away into the *Englisch*
world. As a result, he preferred to avoid that
influence. At least Levy's project would guarantee his men work all summer.

"*Ja*, sure, we'll do it." He knew his tone
sounded unenthusiastic, but he couldn't help it.
Proximity to Eliza still rattled him, and he knew
Levy knew it. "I'll take your plans and work
you up a quote."

"*Danke*, Josiah." Levy stood up. "I'll warn
Eliza ahead of time. She'll keep out of your
way, I'm sure."

Eliza felt the blood drain from her face.
"What do you mean, Josiah will be working
on the house expansion?"

"Just that," replied Levy. "He and his crew
are the only ones available at the moment. If

we don't book them in, we may not get the work done this summer at all. Everyone else is booked solid."

"Levy, you can't." Panic tinged her voice. "It will cause tongues to wag…"

"Don't be dramatic, Eliza." Her brother's face held a note of sternness she hadn't seen since her rebellious adolescent days, when he'd stepped into the role of father after their parents were killed. "You're an adult. He's an adult. Surely you can interact with him as a grown-up, not like some quivering *youngie*."

She drew herself up. "*Ja*, you're right. I'm sorry, Levy. I won't give Josiah any problems, I promise." She tamped down her concerns in an attempt to show Levy how eager she was to be obedient and trusting, but deep inside her stomach turned. Josiah would be here every day. She would have to make sure no one had an excuse to misjudge them.

"*Gut*. I've accepted his quote, so he and his crew will start next week."

Eliza watched as her brother returned to his work outdoors. Something approaching fear clutched at her midsection.

Josiah, here at the house. She knew work on the expansion could take weeks, perhaps months. And during all that time, she would need to maintain her dignity and poise in the presence of the one man in the entire community who still had the ability to unnerve her.

"Please, *Gott*, let me abide by Your will," she whispered. She vowed to behave with the decorum expected of a full church member, even if she wasn't one. She would think of it as just one more piece of preparation for baptism.

The first test of her resolve came later in the afternoon when she heard a knock at the door. Josiah. Eliza went very still for a moment as she composed herself before opening the door. "*Guder nammidaag*, Josiah."

"*Guder nammidaag*." His voice was stiff, distant. He held himself very still. "I hope you don't think I'm happy to be taking this job."

Her temper, never far away, flared up at his blunt remark, and she raised her chin a fraction. "I'm no more happy that you're taking it. But we're going to have to put up with it, Josiah. I can assure you I'll do everything in my power to stay out of your way." Her voice was tart. This was her home. Josiah had no right to insult her right off the bat like that.

Evidently he realized it, too, for he scrubbed a hand over his face in a gesture of weariness. "I'm sorry. That was uncalled for. But *ja*, I think it best if we just avoid each other as much as possible. Is Levy home?"

"He's out back. Come in, I'll call him."

Eliza padded toward the back door, her heart beating fast. He was still as handsome as ever, his dark curly hair and blue eyes just as capable of sending her middle into a tailspin. But his rude tone threw a dark film over her mood.

She walked outside and waded among the corn and tomato plants until she found her brother. "Levy, Josiah is here to see you."

"Ja, danke." He finished tying up a tomato plant, then removed his hat long enough to wipe some sweat off his forehead. He cocked his head at her. "You okay?"

"Ja, sure." She held her head poised, her spine stiff. "I'm being a grown-up, remember?"

Her brother chuckled. *"Gut.* We'll probably need to lay out the plans on the kitchen table and discuss what needs to be done on the house, so consider that a fair warning."

"Ja, I will." Eliza vowed to stay in the living room.

She waited outside a few moments, allowing her brother to invite Josiah into the kitchen, before slipping around the house to the front door, which led directly into the living room. She busied herself sewing the bits together to make the cloth doll Jane had requested, pushing the treadle with her right foot while the machine's needle joined the fabric pieces. But her calm demeanor disguised an oversize reaction to Josiah's close presence.

"*Gott*, keep me calm," she whispered in what was becoming an alarmingly frequent petition.

She heard the men murmuring over the house plans from the next room. They remained there, and she began to relax into her sewing.

That is, until Levy walked into the living room with Josiah on his heels. "I thought a doorway from this room into the new extension might work…" Her brother gestured and pointed.

Eliza blanched. She caught Josiah's eye and turned away, focusing on the pieces of fabric assembling themselves under her fingertips. Nor did she turn back until the two men had gone outside.

She whooshed out her breath and dropped her head into her hands. Weeks. She would have weeks of this, possibly a couple of months. How would she handle it?

After fifteen more minutes of work, when it seemed Levy and Josiah would stay outside, she wandered into the kitchen and made herself a cup of tea. The expansion plans lay spread out on the kitchen table. Eliza bent over them, seeing how the house would almost double in size upon completion, making room for the large brood Jane and Levy no doubt anticipated.

She heard Levy enter the kitchen. "This looks *gut*…" she began, then realized it was not Levy, it was Josiah, coming to collect the sketches and drawings. Levy was nowhere to be seen.

"Danke." He stood there, arms crossed, no smile on his face.

For a moment, silence ricocheted around the kitchen. Finally Eliza took a sip of her tea. "This is going to be awkward, isn't it?"

"Ja." He walked to the table and started rolling up the large sheets of paper. "I think so."

"Levy said there were no other crews available to work on the house."

"He's right. He just happened to catch me at a short downtime, when I could schedule him in." He tapped the sheets together with what seemed unnecessary force. "And believe me, this job doesn't thrill me any more than it thrills you."

"Oh." Pain shot through her and she turned away.

"Faeriwell, Eliza. Tell Levy I'll be ready to start within two or three days."

"Ja, sure, I will. *Faeriwell*."

A moment later the kitchen door opened, then closed, and he was gone.

Eliza released a pent-up breath. She was in for a long summer.

Hearing voices, she saw Jane just coming up the walkway outside. Her sister-in-law paused to speak with Josiah. Unlike the stiff demeanor he affected when he was around her, Josiah smiled and chatted with Jane, perfectly at ease in her company. After a moment, he flicked his hat brim, settled the rolls of paper under his arm and strode off.

Jane came into the kitchen. She took one look at Eliza and said, "What's wrong?"

"Isn't it obvious?" Eliza dropped onto a kitchen chair. "He just walked away, if that's any clue."

"Ach, *lieb*, this is going to be a rough summer for you, isn't it?" Jane placed a basket on the counter and made herself some tea.

"*Ja*, but I promised *Gott* to behave myself. And Levy had a few words with me, as well. He basically told me to stop acting like a *youngie*."

Jane chuckled. "That sounds like Levy."

"He hates me, Jane. He really does." Tears prickled at the backs of her eyes.

"Josiah hates you? No, I'm sure he doesn't…"

"He said this job doesn't thrill him any more than it thrills me. That's what he said."

"The job itself, or its proximity to you?" As usual, Jane's feminine instinct pinpointed the issue.

"Proximity to me. He's fine with the job. I glanced at the *haus* plans, and they look very *gut*, very professional. I'm sure he's an excellent carpenter. But clearly I'm the fly in his ointment."

"Then you'll just have to stay out of his way."

"*Ja*, but that won't be easy. I have work to do, and I live here. No, I've decided I'm not going to cower in my room like a *youngie* with a crush. This is my home. I'm an adult and a mother." Eliza lifted her chin. "Josiah will just have to live with that."

Jane chuckled again and patted her hand. "*Gut* for you."

By the time the work crew started, Eliza had sewn four dolls—two girls, two boys—and outfitted them with tiny clothing. The boys had little black felt hats, and the girls had diminutive bonnets.

She ignored the banging and chatter and laughter of the men as they began tearing off some of the house siding preparatory to framing the new rooms. Her living room doll-making station was interrupted so often that she finally asked Levy to set up a low plywood barrier across the portion of the room holding the sewing machine and table, so she could keep Mercy confined with her while she worked.

"Oh, these are lovely." Jane examined the faceless dolls with interest. "I can almost guarantee they'll sell, every last one. Can you start on more? Perhaps using different colors for the shirts and dresses?"

"*Ja*, sure, I can do that. If this works, it will be my own contribution to the *haus* income. I'd like that."

"And between this and raising Mercy, you won't have time to think of Josiah, is that it?"

"*Ja*, true." She sighed. "I can't believe what a fool I was. If I hadn't left the community, we might be married by now." Being around him made her think of this more and more. It was a torture, a reminder of her missteps.

"Well, he's not married yet."

"That doesn't matter. He doesn't like me, his mother doesn't like me, and I have no intention of opening up a hornet's nest by making another bad choice." Eliza folded some fabric and tucked it away. "I promised *Gott* many things when I returned. One of those things was to behave with the decorum He expects. As far as I'm concerned, Josiah is off my radar."

She would have to work hard to make sure he stayed that way and that the community was aware of her propriety.

From his position in the kitchen modifying a sketch of the expansion, Josiah overheard the entire conversation between Eliza and Jane.

He finished his notes on the house plans and,

without making a noise, left the kitchen to rejoin his crew. The men bantered cheerfully as they worked, and Josiah envied them their peace of mind. They weren't being pulled in two different directions, as he was.

Eliza didn't know it, but his brief association with Jodie was over. Already his mother was trying to interest him in someone else, a wearying practice he wished she would stop. Despite everything his mother said on the matter, he wasn't ready to get married.

His mother. Josiah sighed. As the youngest son, it was his duty to support his mother, especially in her widowed state. But sometimes she nagged too much…especially in matters that were none of her concern.

He swung a hammer and thought about Eliza. Yes, she'd gone through her rebellious phase. Yes, she'd left her church community and had some wild adventures out in the *Englisch* world. Yes, she had a baby. But she was different now—penitent of her flaws, determined not to make additional mistakes, anxious to become a strong contributor to the community. He wasn't sure, but he suspected some in the community talked ill of her, and he knew she was trying hard not to fuel any gossip.

He tried not to think about her attractions—

that inner core of steel, the innate dignity, even her whip-fast temper.

But that streak of rebellion… His mother never ceased to tell him a rebellious woman did not make a good wife. Marriage was forever, and a woman like Eliza could be trouble in the future, his mother continually pointed out. Ruby seemed curiously insistent on that point.

Whatever the reason, he wasn't anxious to cause a rift with his mother. Josiah cherished his remaining parent and took seriously his responsibility of caring for her after his father died. He didn't want to cause bad feelings between them.

He shifted two-by-four pieces of wood with his men, building the framework of a new room, hammering and sawing and bracing, but his mind wasn't on his work. Instead, it was on the contrite woman just on the other side of the wall, sewing gewgaws to sell at a farmers market and help provide income for her brother's household.

He prayed for forgiveness for his own rebellious spirit, the love and anger that warred within him. It wasn't an easy battle, and he wondered which side would win. Maybe, just maybe, he should take his mother's advice and start looking in earnest for a bride. That might be the only thing that would wipe Eliza from his heart.

Chapter Three

~

Late on Saturday afternoon, Eliza heard the clip-clop of hooves and went to the door. She saw Levy and Jane returning from their day of selling at the farmers market. Both their shoulders drooped with weariness.

But Jane broke into a smile when she saw Eliza. "They sold out."

"Everything?"

"Everything. All four dolls."

"Gut." Eliza kept her expression calm, but inside she was leaping with glee. Everything sold! She now could help earn her keep. And it would also mean she had work which would keep her mind off Josiah.

"Looks like you now have a business," said Levy. He swung down from the wagon and turned to assist Jane. "You can make as many dolls as you want, and I suspect we'll sell them all."

"*Ja*, sure. I have more dolls cut out already, but I need to pick up more batting this week." She went out to help carry items from the wagon, and her curiosity got the better of her. "Who bought the toys?"

"A grandmother bought one pair, a young mother with a baby son bought one of the boy dolls, and the last girl doll was bought by a man." Jane's brow furrowed. "He was *Englisch*, and he seemed especially interested in the dolls, I don't know why. He asked if I made them, but I said no, you were the maker. He said he might want to talk to you about them someday."

"Talk to me about dolls? I wonder why."

"I don't know, but he was very intense, very insistent."

Eliza soon forgot about the insistent man and instead thanked *Gott* she was able to contribute to the household income.

"*Ach*, this is one nice thing about having you home," sighed Levy later as he dropped onto a kitchen chair. "A meal already made."

"Just one nice thing?" Eliza teased from the stove where she was dishing up food, and Levy grinned at her.

"Last summer, before you came home, we were so busy," added Jane, as she seated Mercy in her high chair. "On Saturday evenings, we'd get home late and had no food made for dinner." She, too, sat down. "Those were long days."

"And you were taking care of my baby." Eliza touched her daughter's hair, then brought dinner to the table. "I don't know how you did it, how you managed to make everything to sell while taking care of her."

"I set myself a weekly schedule," explained Jane. "On Mondays I did one thing, on Tuesdays I did another. Things that needed to be freshest for selling at the farmers market, such as the baked goods, I made later in the week. It worked out well, and Mercy was young enough to be in a sling most of the time, so she wasn't much trouble. But it's nice to come in to a meal already made."

"I'd like to go to the farmers market one day," admitted Eliza. "I'm curious. I've never seen the booth open for business."

"We can swap some time, if you like," offered Jane. "I'll stay home with Mercy, and you can help Levy."

"*Ja!* I'd like that."

On Monday, Levy announced, "I need to go to town for some items. Eliza, what was it you said you needed?"

"Stuffing for the dolls." Eliza fished out a

sample bit of poly fill from her work area. "I could use a lot, many bags of it."

"There's a fabric store in town. I'll ask there."

"Danke."

Over the din of hammers and talking men, Eliza laid out fabric on the sewing table and cut out doll parts. Eliza brought Mercy into what she was referring to as her sewing station—a low barricaded section of the living room Levy had rigged up for her with plywood, where her baby could play and explore at her mother's feet. Crew members came in and out of the house, gesturing, measuring, ripping, nailing. Once, Eliza met Josiah's eye, but she turned away. His shirt was damp, he had a fine sheen of sawdust adhering to his clothes, and his appearance affected her more than she wanted to admit. Best not to look at him at all.

But it wasn't easy to concentrate. The living room was now the focus of the construction project. One whole wall of the house was off as the workmen hammered and framed the new rooms. Josiah was everywhere—directing the other men, consulting the plans, measuring, sawing, pounding nails into boards.

While the open wall provided a lovely view of the garden in back, Eliza felt very exposed as the men worked. She kept her head bent over her sewing. She could feel Josiah's eyes on her and refused to look his way.

Mercy seemed unfazed by the noise and commotion of the house expansion. But she grew fussy in the afternoon, her usual nap time, so Eliza prepared a bottle of formula and settled into the rocking chair with the baby. She closed her eyes as she fed her daughter, unwilling to risk looking at Josiah. After the baby fell asleep, Eliza laid her down in a crib off the kitchen and returned to work.

"You've gotten a lot done," commented Jane, wandering by.

"You'd be surprised how hard I'm concentrating," admitted Eliza, jerking her head a bit toward the work crew.

She knew her sister-in-law understood. "Will you be able to do this here, with all this noise?" Jane asked. "I can set you up to do sewing at my aunt and uncle's *haus*, if that will help."

"And run away like a coward? No." Eliza traced another pattern on the fabric. "This is my home. I refuse to leave just because I can't control my emotions toward a man I left behind. Think of it as a sort of penance."

"As you say." Jane looked unhappy, but she didn't press.

Eliza's heart warmed toward her sister-in-law. "I'll let you know if I need to get away," she said.

Eliza's hard-won composure was challenged the next day shortly before lunch when Josiah spoke to her. The workmen were on the other side of the house and he was by himself for a moment. "You're always sewing. What are you making?"

Eliza bit her lip, fighting her physical reaction to his simple question. She kept her face blank and her voice neutral. "Dolls. I made one for Mercy, and Jane and Levy thought they would sell well at the farmers market. It seems they're right, so now I'm making more."

"That's *gut.*" He slipped his hammer into his tool belt. "I'm glad you have a sideline business."

"Why?" She eyed him with something approaching suspicion.

"Because it will…" His voice died out.

"Because it will keep me from getting into more trouble, is that what you were going to say?"

"No! That wasn't what I was going to say at all."

"*Gut.* Because I can assure you, Josiah, I will never get myself into trouble again." Eliza turned back to her work.

"Because it will help restore your confidence." He spoke quietly. "That's what I was going to say."

"Oh." Eliza paused. Her defensive anger died and she felt her cheeks grow warm. Clearly she still had a long way to go to forgive herself, and here she was projecting her insecurity onto Josiah. "I'm sorry, then. I shouldn't have bitten your head off."

He nodded at her apology. Eliza looked at him, square in the eye, something she had avoided doing for so long. His expression was warm and interested, and for just a moment she allowed herself the fantasy of wondering…

"Josiah?" A soft voice spoke behind him.

He whirled. A young woman stood there, a picnic basket in her hand. "*Guder mariye*, Maggie."

"*Guder mariye.*" The pretty girl smiled. "I brought lunch. I thought you'd like to eat outside under the maple tree."

"*Ja, gut. Danke.*"

Eliza saw him flick her a glance before he followed the young woman outside. She also noticed that the woman herself shot her a look that was more suspicious than friendly.

Maggie? Who was she? Eliza turned back to her sewing and tears blurred her eyes. Whoever Maggie was—probably Ruby's latest selection for her son—*Gott* had sent her just at that moment, Eliza was sure. *Gott* was reminding her of her promise not to interfere in Josiah's love life.

Mercy let out a wail as she woke up from her nap. Glad for an excuse to stop focusing on the couple now sitting under the maple tree, Eliza picked up her sleepy daughter and went into the kitchen to prepare another bottle of formula. She sat in the rocking chair and fed Mercy, feeling the precious weight of her daughter in her arms.

This is enough, she thought. *Raising my daughter to be a good woman, unlike the way I was—it's enough.*

"So if you could begin stocking what I'll need for my doll business, I can get it directly from you," concluded Eliza.

Jane's uncle Peter and aunt Catherine owned a dry-goods store nearby, and Eliza had decided to work through them to supply her with what she needed to sew more dolls.

"*Ja*, sure, we can do that." Peter made notations on a pad of paper. "Give me a list of things you need."

"And let me take the baby." Catherine's motherly face lit up as she slipped the young toddler into her arms. "Ach, *liebling*, how you've grown…"

Eliza smiled as the older woman fussed over

her baby, then turned back to Peter. "I'll need batting on a regular basis," she said, and mentioned her preferred brand. "Also, bolts of cotton fabric in various colors. If you can order them wholesale, I'll take the whole bolt rather than buying it by the yard…"

"We can purchase everything you need wholesale," offered Peter, "and then sell it to you with no markup."

"Oh no, that's not fair! Make yourself a profit."

"Our profit will be watching your business grow." Peter waved a hand. "I insist. You're family now."

Eliza felt her eyes prickle at the older man's kindness. "*Danke*, Peter. I'm grateful."

"Besides, we'd like to stock some of your dolls here in the store. We don't carry any right now, and tourists always want some," he added.

"*Ja*, I'd be happy to!" She shook her head in amazement. "In just one week, I suddenly have a business. It's hard to get used to."

"You've changed so much in the last few years," observed Peter. "We're so happy you're back."

"So is Mercy," added Catherine. She bent over and helped the toddler walk without bumping into things. "From the moment Jane started taking care of this *liebling*, she fell in love with her. Now it's like Mercy has two mothers."

"I love your niece like she's my own sister."
Eliza leaned on the counter near the cash register. "*Gott* blessed Levy when he married her.
And soon she'll have her own baby."

"*Ja, Gott ist gut.*" Catherine picked up Mercy
and handed her back to her mother.

"Come, *liebling*, let's go home." Eliza slipped
the toddler into a cloth sling, settled her on her
hip and thanked the Troyers once again. She felt
a warm glow of gratitude toward Jane's aunt and
uncle for their staunch support.

She opened the store's front door and stepped
outside onto the wooden porch of the building—
and came face-to-face with Ruby, carrying a
large basket covered with a cloth.

Determined to be pleasant to the older
woman, Eliza smiled. "*Guder nammidaag*,
Ruby. Doing a bit of shopping?"

The older woman paused. She didn't smile,
but at least her voice was not hostile. "No, bringing some baby quilts." She touched the basket.
"The Troyers sell them for me."

"Oh." Eliza didn't know about this sideline
business. An awkward pause occurred as Eliza
tried to think of something to say. "I've just
been working with Peter Troyer to purchase
some wholesale fabric supplies," she offered.
"I've started a business making dolls. Levy is
selling them at the farmers market."

Perhaps it was her imagination, but she thought she saw a flash of disdain on Ruby's face before it smoothed away. "*Ja, gut.* At least you haven't forgotten how to sew."

The small dig grated, but Eliza kept a smile on her face. "No. And I'm getting better, too." She shifted Mercy in her sling. Ruby made no reference to her baby either, which bothered Eliza for some reason. "Well, I hope you sell a lot of quilts. *Faeriwell.*"

She descended the steps from the store and walked home, thinking about Ruby and wondering how to fix her hostility. There was nothing she could do, she concluded, except steer clear of Josiah…which she planned to do anyway.

"I must say, you're pouring heart and soul into this new business of yours." Jane surveyed the inventory of dolls clustered in several large baskets. "How many were you able to make this week?"

"Twenty sets, forty dolls in all. I'll drop five sets off with your aunt and uncle to sell at the store, and the rest can go with you and Levy tomorrow to the farmers market." Eliza pushed a strand of hair that escaped her *kapp* back into place, and blew out a breath. "I'm a bit tired," she admitted. "Forty dolls in one week is quite a lot."

"I can see why, even though you've got the assembly-line technique going well."

"I'm going to start another batch today, though. If I work today and tomorrow, I'll get a head start over what I was able to do this past week." Eliza scrubbed a hand down her face. "If I work around Mercy's naps and bedtime, I can probably make fifty dolls a week, but I think that's the most I can do."

"Don't burn yourself out."

"I won't. I just have to get into the groove, that's all. Just like you do with making jams and chutneys and baked goods for the farmers market. Perhaps I should set myself a weekly schedule, where I do one task per day—cut out the forms, or make the clothes, or whatever."

"The popularity of the dolls may not last," warned Jane. "That's the thing I've noticed about the farmers market. Nonfood items have cycles. Your dolls will be the hottest thing going for a while, but when everyone who wants one has one, sales will drop dramatically. Uncle Peter and Aunt Catherine's store will probably be a more reliable outlet in the long term. So after a few weeks of hard work, you can probably go a little easier."

"*Ja, gut.* But during those few weeks, at least I'm contributing to the household income."

* * *

The following morning, Eliza helped her brother and sister-in-law pack the wagon to the brim with the booth and the inventory to sell at the farmers market. She waved goodbye and watched the loaded vehicle clip-clop down the road. Then she turned to go back into the house.

She and Mercy were by themselves for the day. Eliza had fallen into an efficient schedule in which she could care for her baby as well as sew, and she took advantage of it now since Mercy was still in bed.

She laid out fabric, traced the patterns and cut out doll parts. She got a great deal done before she heard Mercy's cries when she woke up.

"Ach, *liebling*, hush, hush…" she crooned as she lifted her sleepy daughter out of the crib. She changed her diaper and settled into the rocking chair with a bottle of formula, singing a soft song to the child. She was so absorbed in tenderly caring for Mercy that she shut out the world around them.

"Oh. You're here."

Eliza whipped her head up. Josiah stood in the framed expansion of the house, tool belt around his waist and hammer in hand. Eliza's heart kallumped in her chest at seeing him.

"*Ja*, of course," she replied, striving to keep her voice calm.

"I thought you went with Levy and Jane to the farmers market."

"No, I have sewing to do. I might go next week, but today I'm working here." She paused. "But what are you doing here without your crew? It's Saturday."

"I told Levy I wanted to get some windows installed. I don't need the crew for that, and it would put us ahead for Monday." He fiddled with his hammer.

"Well, go ahead." Her voice was clipped. "I won't interfere. I have my own work to do."

He met her eyes for a long moment, then nodded. "Well, then."

Flustered, Eliza got out of the rocking chair and stepped over the little barrier Levy had made to confine Mercy to her sewing area. She put the child down on the floor and gave her toys to play with while she continued cutting out doll parts.

But with Josiah working just in the next room, her concentration was shot. She felt self-conscious, as if his eyes were on her, but she refused to look up to confirm her suspicions.

When noon approached, Eliza wondered if she should prepare food for Josiah as well as herself. Well, she would prepare a meal. If Josiah was hungry, she would offer him some, but nothing said she had to sit with him at the table.

"I'll be gone just a moment, *liebling*," she told Mercy. "Stay here until *Mamm* gets back." Stepping back over the barrier, Eliza went into the basement to fetch a jar of canned corn for the lunch meal.

From above, she heard a thump and her baby's cry. Eliza gasped, gathered her skirts and dashed up the basement stairs.

But Josiah had reached Mercy first. He held her against his chest, crooning to the baby. "There, there, you didn't get hurt…"

"What happened?" she panted.

"I think she was pulling herself up on the sewing table and knocked something over." Josiah didn't seem in any hurry to hand the baby over. He swayed with Mercy's cheek against his chest, and the baby stopped crying. "She's a pretty thing," he admitted.

"*Ja*, she is." Eliza wondered if Josiah was thinking the same thing she was—that if Eliza hadn't left when she did, Mercy might be their child. "You're *gut* with babies."

"Who doesn't like babies?" He continued to sway the child.

"Maybe you'll have some of your own someday." There. She said it.

Josiah kept his eyes on the top of Mercy's head. "*Ja*. No doubt." At last he held out the baby. "Here, I think she wants you."

The act of transferring the child led inevitably toward physical contact. Eliza didn't like the sparks that seemed to snap off his skin as she took Mercy into her arms. "I'm making corn casserole for lunch if you get hungry."

"Ja, danke." He backed up. *"Danke."* He turned and fled into the construction zone.

Eliza stared after him.

Josiah returned to work, flustered. Oddly, it wasn't just Eliza who disturbed him—it was the baby. The feel of the child nestled against his chest awoke in him a sharp longing.

Most men his age were already fathers. One by one, his boyhood cohort had taken vows, grown their beards to proclaim their married status and, within a year or two, had the beginnings of a family. All except him.

He found it unusual that little Mercy had let him hold her without struggle. He knew toddlers were often wary of strangers, but she had turned to him for comfort without complaint. He found himself strangely moved by the incident.

He wondered if Eliza thought what now passed through his mind—that if she hadn't left when she did, Mercy might be their child.

He had to shake those thoughts free. His lunch the other day with Maggie had been pleasant, and he knew she'd look kindly on another invitation to see each other. Even if she didn't affect him the way Eliza did, he could still be someone's husband, dutiful and kind. Besides, if he showed interest in other women, it would be good for Eliza, too. It would stifle gossip they were reconnecting in any way.

Chapter Four

"There's a *youngie* event over at the Herschbergers' tonight if you want to go," Jane said. "I'd be happy to watch Mercy for you."

Eliza looked up from her sewing. "Why would I go to a *youngie* event?"

"Because you're young and single. Why wouldn't you?"

"I don't feel young, and I don't feel single." Eliza gestured toward Mercy, who was stumbling around, trying out her new skill of walking. "I'm a mother."

"*Ja*, sure, but you've also been too serious." Jane lifted Mercy into her arms and cooed at the toddler. "You spend hours and hours every day sewing, and the rest of your time is taken up with caring for Mercy. Don't you think you deserve a little time off? Besides—" Jane bobbed her eyebrows "—all the single young men will be there. Maybe you'll meet someone."

Eliza gave a bitter laugh. "Who would be interested? I'm damaged goods."

"Ah, *lieb*, don't call yourself that." Jane looked distressed. "Trust *Gott* to work things out for you. He did for me."

"You didn't rebel and leave the community, as I did." As she looked back on that time, it felt more and more as if she'd deliberately turned away from *Gott*. While it was an issue she needed to work out with *Gott* alone, she understood how there were those who passed judgment on her because of it.

"No, but I was convinced no one could ever love me. I was Plain Jane. Your brother was able to see below the surface and find the lonely woman underneath, and we've never been happier. *Gott* has ways of making things work out. Besides—" Jane gave Mercy a gentle bounce "—this little one has been a blessing. Don't beat yourself up for how she came to be. The important thing is, she's here for all of us to love."

Eliza was heartened by her sister-in-law's words. She leaned over and kissed the other woman on the cheek. "It's easy to see why Levy loves you so much. *Ja*, I'll go to the *youngie* event. You're right, I should probably get out."

* * *

All the single young men. Eliza walked toward the Herschbergers', carrying a basket packed with goodies. She knew Jane meant well in encouraging her to attend *youngie* functions, but Eliza couldn't see how any single young man could overlook the stigma of her rebellious past and the burden of a toddler to court her. She shrugged. As *Gott* wills.

The Herschbergers' yard was swarming with young people, with colorful shirts and dresses bright against the grass. Trying not to feel self-conscious, Eliza carried her basket to the trestle tables set up under the shade of some generous maple trees, and unpacked her share of the food.

The *youngies* clustered around a long trench at the edge of the yard in which embers glowed and flames licked logs spread along it. People held out metal pronged holders with hot dogs or marshmallows, roasting them over the heat. They laughed and chattered. Snatches of song rose.

Eliza stood with her back to a tree and watched. She felt detached from the happy *youngies*, who looked like they didn't have a care in the world. She could tell, from the quick glances and frowns, that at least some in the crowd still viewed her as an outsider, maybe even someone to stay away from. She didn't feel like socializing and wished she hadn't come.

And then she saw them. Squeezed in among the laughing, joking group, Josiah and another young woman stood on the edge of the trench and roasted hot dogs over the embers. His companion, whoever she was, looked young and pretty and vivacious. The sight brought Eliza a stab of pain.

She turned and saw Catherine Troyer—Jane's aunt—sitting in a chair under a tree, benevolently watching the group. She walked over. "May I join you?"

"Of course." The older woman gestured toward a nearby chair, and Eliza pulled it over.

"Danke."

"Aren't you hungry? There's lots of food."

"Maybe in a while."

With feminine instinct, Catherine asked, "Is it awkward, being here with the other *youngies* when you're a mother?"

"Ja." Eliza felt relief that Catherine understood. "I feel so much older than everyone, even though most are about my age."

"That's what comes with motherhood. You're at that uneasy in-between state, *ja*? You're unmarried, but you're also a mother and have more responsibility than all the *youngies*."

"That's it exactly. You always were a wise woman, Catherine."

"That's because I understand precisely what you've been through, *lieb*. I had a rebellious past, too."

"You?" Eliza stared.

"*Ja*, me. I won't go into details because it still makes me ashamed. All I'll say is it took utter faith in *Gott* to straighten myself out. Peter—" she nodded at her husband, chatting a distance away with some other men "—he knew what kind of trouble I got into, but he knew I was serious about changing and turning my life over to *Gott*."

"What..." Eliza's voice came out as a croak. In all the years she'd known Catherine, no hint of scandal had ever touched her, no indication she had ever been anything but a devout, productive member of the community. "Never mind, I don't want to know what you did." She took a breath that shook a bit. "I just never would have guessed it, is all."

"There are more of us around than you think," observed Catherine. "A fair number of us older women have done something we're ashamed of. I'm not going to name names, of course, but I want you to remember that—a number of us older women have done something we're ashamed of."

Eliza stared at Catherine. "That almost sounds like a warning."

"Not a warning, exactly...just some words of advice. I want you to remember what I'm saying, because something tells me it may be useful to you someday."

"Catherine, you're talking in riddles."

The older woman smiled. "That's because I don't want to indulge in the sin of gossip. So I'll only repeat it once more—a number of us older women have something in our past we're not proud of. Remember that."

What a curiously intense point to emphasize, thought Eliza. "I will, thank you." She tried to extract a moral from Catherine's point. "And I guess it means someday this will all be behind me."

"*Ja*, it will. You have to realize, child, that rebellious youth only lasts a short time. Adulthood lasts the rest of your life. No one can change the past. The only thing we can change is the future, and that change comes from making *gut* choices. You made a *gut* choice by coming home. Hopefully, you'll make the choice to be baptized. But whatever you choose, it seems you've been doing fine since you got home."

"I've tried." Eliza's gaze strayed toward Josiah and his pretty companion before she looked at the ground. "It hasn't been easy, but I've tried."

She knew Catherine had picked up the glance and guessed its significance. "Are you still interested in Josiah?"

"No!" Her protest came too fast. She saw Catherine raise an eyebrow. "Okay, maybe it's hard to get him out of my heart," she amended. "But it doesn't matter. Josiah doesn't like me, and neither does Ruby, his mother."

"And I assume you don't like Ruby?"

"Maybe." Eliza fiddled with the string of her *kapp*. She knew she could be honest with Catherine. "I know she didn't approve of my coming back, and I think it stemmed from how I treated her son."

"And now her son is seeing a variety of women." Catherine's voice stayed bland. "But he's not courting any of them."

"Josiah can do whatever he wants," retorted Eliza with asperity. "I've promised *Gott* not to interfere in any way. Let him marry whomever he wants. I can't and won't object." She heard the jangling note of bitterness in her voice.

"I think you're exaggerating your history. You may have made poor choices in the past, but *Gott* in His wisdom gives us the chance to make *gut* choices in the future. If you remember that and let it guide you, you'll do fine."

Eliza sighed. "So what should I do, Catherine?" Though it was good to confide in the woman, it just brought her misery to the surface.

"Precisely what you're currently doing. You said you promised *Gott* not to interfere with Josiah's personal life. Keep to that promise. *Gott* will decide the future, and if you've conducted yourself with dignity and self-control, then no one can blame you, whatever may happen."

Whatever may happen. Later, as Eliza walked home in the darkness, swinging the empty basket, she wondered what Catherine suspected. The older woman's cryptic hint about some mysterious scandal in her own past—and her insistence that Eliza remember that—was interesting.

The stars shone overhead and a warm breeze breathed across her face. Eliza watched the fireflies sparkle in the fields, saw the dim twinkle of kerosene lamps in various distant homes, and thanked *Gott* to be back among her people. She was glad Mercy would be raised in the church community, not struggling as the daughter of a single mother out in the *Englisch* world.

And here, Eliza had the support of others. Yes, Ruby Lapp didn't approve of her, but what did it matter? She was just one person. Everyone else had been welcoming and nonjudgmental about her decision to return to the community.

A faint crunch of feet on gravel ahead made her look up. In the darkness, she saw the form of a man approaching, wearing an Amish straw hat. Not sure who it was, she said, *"Gut'n owed."*

"Gut'n owed, Eliza."

It was Josiah. Of all the people to meet alone on a dark road, it was Josiah. Eliza gritted her teeth and recalled her promise to *Gott*. She prayed for self-control and dignity, just as Catherine had suggested. And she hoped no one was around to see them together and get the wrong impression.

"Heading home?" she asked in a neutral voice.

"Ja. I just walked Marion back to her house."

Marion. So that was the name of his unknown companion. In the dim starlight, Eliza could not see the expression on Josiah's face. Determined that everything she said would be guided by *Gott*, she complimented him. "She seems like a *gut* woman."

"Ja, sure." Josiah took off his hat and ran a hand through his hair, before replacing it back on his head. "She's a *gut* woman, all right."

Surprised at the lack of enthusiasm in his voice, she blurted, "But you spent the whole evening with her!"

"Ja, and then I walked her home. Eliza, we

are alone on a dark road. Are we going to do nothing but make polite chitchat about Marion?"

Startled, she actually stepped back. "What do you mean?"

"I mean, maybe we should talk about *you*."

This was the last thing Eliza expected. "What is there to say?"

"I could say something about how much I'm impressed with what you've done since returning to the community."

"Danke." She squinted at him with suspicion. She didn't like the turn this conversation had taken, not with her promise to *Gott* fresh in her mind.

"Can I walk you home, too? It's awfully dark out here." He reached for her basket.

"No." She stepped back again. "That wouldn't be appropriate, Josiah. And you know that."

"Maybe I do." His voice was hoarse. "And maybe I don't care."

"Well, I do care. You've done nothing but give me the cold shoulder since I returned home. To change tactics all of a sudden makes me suspicious. I see you with a dazzling number of pretty young women, all of whom are respectable. Just pick one, would you?" She was glad it was dark and he couldn't see her face warming with blush and her eyes blinking back tears.

"Pick one?" His voice was heavy with sarcasm.

"*Ja*, pick one. Or don't. I don't care. Just leave me out of it."

"But what if I don't want to?" he blurted.

"You're a *dumkupp*, Josiah." She shook her head. "Don't do the wrong thing. And I have no intention of being the wrong thing. *Gute nacht*."

She sidestepped him and continued down the road.

Tears blurred her eyes. Why oh why had *Gott* allowed her to meet with Josiah on a dark road? It was the perfect setup for romantic sparks to fly, and above all Eliza didn't want those sparks. She didn't. She was sure she didn't. She was definitely sure she didn't want anything flaring up with Josiah if it meant nothing more than a passing fancy on his way to marriage to another woman.

But like a sore tooth, she kept returning to what he said. *What if I don't want to?*

Want to what? Marry any of the young women she'd seen him with?

Why would he suddenly open up to her? They'd barely exchanged words since her return. She tried to hold herself aloof, tried not to show her interest in Josiah, tried to give him the space and support to court someone, anyone. Why couldn't he do the same, and give her the space she needed?

Among the Amish, marriages were forever.

As a result, young people had to be sure they were marrying the right person. Since they already matched on such critical matters of faith, family and finances, it was then a simple matter to find someone with whom one was personally compatible. If Josiah wasn't eager to wed anyone, was she—Eliza—the cause?

Eliza allowed her thoughts to stray to Bill, the *Englisch* man she had married after a whirlwind courtship when she had left the Amish four years ago. In the stupid blindness of youth, she saw him only as wild and exciting. She didn't consider the importance of faith, family and finances. She saw only how handsome he was, how different from the usual Amish men she'd grown up with. How opposite he was of someone as responsible and hardworking as Josiah.

It took about two weeks after the courthouse wedding for her to recognize the mistake she'd made. Bill had no interest in settling down and being a mature, responsible husband or father. He just wanted to continue his fast-paced, party-hard lifestyle. She realized how naive she'd been in thinking he would change after the marriage vows were spoken.

And when she became pregnant shortly thereafter, Bill had been unenthusiastic—even hostile—to the notion of fatherhood. He urged her over and over to make an unspeakable choice about the baby, but Eliza refused. Deep down she knew it was just a matter of time before Bill would abandon her and her unborn child.

And then came that fateful and horrible day when, after an argument, he grabbed the car keys and sped away. She clearly remembered the sympathetic eyes of the police officer who came to her door to tell her the news of the crash.

She didn't mourn Bill, but she mourned her own stupidity. She felt guilt over her relief to be freed from him. But it also meant she was widowed and pregnant in a huge city, far from home, working a minimum-wage job, living in a tiny, cheap apartment. What had she done? How had she managed to mess up her life so badly?

And when little Mercy was born, she knew she couldn't care for the precious infant on her own. That's why she sent her to the only person she trusted, her brother, Levy. Then Levy hired Jane to care for the infant, he fell in love with Jane, and the rest was history.

She thought about what Catherine Troyer had said at this evening's *youngie* event, about the importance of making good choices in life. Until she returned to her Amish community, she had made astoundingly poor choices with lifelong repercussions.

And she thought with profound gratitude

about the *Englisch* pastor and his wife who had found her weeping in their empty Seattle church one afternoon. She ended up confessing everything to them. They had urged her to return to her people, then paid for her return journey here to Grand Creek. Above all, they insisted she shouldn't repay them the travel costs. Instead, they told her to "pay it forward" to someone else who might need help one day. Eliza had vowed she would do just that.

That opportunity—to pay it forward—had not yet arisen, but she was on the lookout for it. It was a debt of gratitude she was eager to fulfill. Maybe her way to pay it forward was to let Josiah go, to make it even clearer he was free to marry, that she wanted him to marry.

The thought made her catch her breath and tears return anew.

She sighed and lifted her eyes to the bright stars overhead. Whatever complex feelings she had about Josiah, they were nothing next to her gratitude to be back home. The things that had happened—having Mercy, sending her to Levy to raise, Levy's hiring Jane as a nanny and then falling in love with her, and Jane becoming her beloved sister-in-law—well, she could see *Gott*'s hand in it all.

She would wait—quietly and with dignity— to see where *Gott*'s hand led her in the future.

* * *

Josiah didn't raise his eyes to the stars. Instead, he kept them on the dark road before him. His mind was filled with gloomy, confusing, irrational thoughts.

Eliza had urged him to leave her alone and focus on someone else. His mother said much the same thing, and provided what seemed like an endless series of "someone elses" to tempt him. So why did every nerve in his body cry out against picking one?

The bland sweetness of Jodie, Maggie and Marion got on his nerves. They tended to have the same attitude: unwavering devotion, the same constant attention and the same expectation that his interest would sharpen into courtship.

But it didn't. He just couldn't put his heart and soul into developing a stronger interest in any of the women his mother suggested. Why? Was it because he still wanted Eliza? He gave a small snort at the thought of what his mother would say to such a decision.

Eliza, he was reminded in no uncertain terms by his mother, was not a respectable woman. In Ruby's eyes, it didn't matter that Eliza had turned over a new leaf. It didn't matter that she had left her past behind. It didn't matter that not a hint of scandal had touched her since she'd returned to Grand Creek. All that mattered, apparently, was that *Eliza was Eliza.*

For just a moment he wondered why his mother was so fixated on Eliza as the arch nemesis. Ruby's vendetta against Eliza seemed based on something deeper.

It was an uncomfortable thing to admit that the women he'd been dating bored him. They hardly had an original thought in their heads, whereas he, Josiah, was constantly thinking about ways to improve his construction business, how to better develop the kitchen garden behind his house and endless other projects. His brain was vibrant, focused and experimental. Jodie, Maggie and Marion were quiet, docile and uninquisitive. And so they bored him.

By contrast, he admired Eliza's spunk, her willingness to stare down the opposition in the community, her devotion to Mercy and her gutsiness to start her own sewing business. He'd noticed how raw her fingers looked from sewing so many dolls, and how tired her eyes had seemed.

He couldn't stop himself from watching her when she was around.

In his confusion over his feelings for her, he knew he'd treated her coldly since her return. At that thought, he stubbed his toe on a rock in the road, and in irritation he picked it up and flung it away. Deep down, he resented his mother's unwavering dislike of Eliza. He was a grown man and shouldn't be worrying about his mother's opinion.

But he also knew his mother was still fragile after the loss of her husband, his father. It seemed her focus on finding someone for him to marry—anyone but Eliza—was somehow connected to her grief over widowhood. This might be *Gott*'s will, for him to tend to his mother's feelings.

Therefore he was, he realized with annoyance, between the proverbial rock and a hard place—and he didn't like it.

As he finished his walk home, he heard laughter ripple in the distance, others heading to their houses. He hoped no one had overheard his talk with Eliza or seen them alone together. That was the last thing she needed.

Chapter Five

"So she's pushing me," concluded Josiah.

"That doesn't seem right."

"It's not. I find myself very annoyed about it, too."

Eliza perked up her ears. Josiah and one of his crew members were talking. She heard them over the banging of hammers as work progressed on the house expansion.

The two men were on the upper floor of the unfinished structure. Curious, Eliza tiptoed into the raw-wood lower portion and eavesdropped on the conversation taking place over her head.

"It's not right," Josiah repeated. "I mean, they've all been very nice women and everything, but why would my mother be pushing me? Isn't it for me to decide?" *Bang bang bang.*

"*Ja,*" replied the unseen crew member. "It's not *gut* to get tangled with the wrong woman.

I knew when I married my Katla she was the only one for me. Marriage is for the rest of your life. You have to be sure."

"That's what I think. And it bothers me that my own mother is trying to play matchmaker." *Bang bang bang.* "After all, I'm the one who's going to have to live with the decision, ain't so?"

"*Ja.* But why is she pushing? Why does she care who you marry? As long as it's within the church community."

"I don't know. There's something about it that seems odd, desperate."

"Well, if you haven't found the right woman yet, don't give in," advised the other man. "That's all there is to it. On the other hand, there are lots of pretty women in the church. Are you even looking?"

There was a pause amid the din of hammers. "Not very much," admitted Josiah. "I'm trying to follow *Gott*'s will, and so far no one seems right."

"Well, there's plenty of time," concluded the crewman.

The sound of hammering ceased, and Eliza heard boot steps from above as the men moved to a different task. She snuck back into the living room and sat down at the treadle sewing machine while Mercy played with fabric scraps at her feet.

But her hands stayed idle. Josiah's conversation with the unseen crew member echoed what he'd said the other night after they met on the dark road. So he "wasn't looking" at any of the other women in the church community. By this point, Eliza knew why.

What she hadn't realized was how hard Ruby was playing matchmaker and pushing her own son into courting someone, anyone—as long as it wasn't her. But the unseen workman was right. Marriage was forever. Marrying the wrong person would be devastating.

She should know.

Eliza stared at her sewing with hot eyes. Settling back among her people after such a long absence—and a degree from the School of Hard Knocks—she knew she would be the subject of speculation, even gossip. Gossip was a sin, and a grievous one, but that didn't prevent people from indulging in it. Perhaps that's why she was so determined to lead as blameless a life as possible, to avoid unwanted speculation about her motives, her emotions or her intentions.

What she hadn't anticipated was how strong her feelings still were for Josiah—or the opposition she would get from his mother.

For a moment she toyed with the idea of leaving the community to avoid causing further problems. She wasn't baptized. She was free to go or do anything she wanted. Would leaving help Josiah stop focusing on her and settle on a more suitable woman? Is that what *Gott* wanted her to do?

But one glance at the content toddler at her feet changed her mind. She'd left once, and it only created more problems—for her brother, for Josiah and for herself. There was no way she would jeopardize the safety and happiness of her tiny daughter just because Josiah was having issues.

Suddenly she was angry. She had done nothing wrong since returning to the community. She had promised *Gott* not to take a step that wasn't guided by Him. If Josiah was being pressured by his mother about his love life—well, that was his problem, not hers.

She yanked fabric pieces toward her and started sewing them together, her movements clipped and annoyed.

Jane came into the room. "I'm going to make some tea. I need to get off my feet for a few minutes," she said. "Do you want some?"

"*Ja*, sure." Eliza glanced at Jane. With her growing pregnancy, her sister-in-law's ankles were swollen, which hardly slowed down the massive work schedule she set for herself every week. Jane's middle was larger, but not by much, though she had taken to wearing looser-fitting dresses.

"Are you much tired?" Eliza picked up the toddler and stepped over the barrier in the living room that cordoned off her sewing station. She followed Jane into the kitchen. "I remember how exhausted I got when I was carrying Mercy."

"*Ja.* I'm a little more tired than I thought I would be." Jane put the kettle on the stove, then collapsed onto a chair. The kitchen was strewn with all the accoutrements for making raspberry jam, Jane's project for the day. "But I'll get through this summer. The *boppli* isn't due until December, so the work schedule will slow down by the time I get really big." She grinned.

"I always thought you were amazing. From what Levy told me about last summer, when you were caring for Mercy as well as making all the items to sell at the farmers market, I couldn't understand how you got it done."

"Well, you're doing much the same thing—watching an active toddler while making items to sell at the market."

"*Ja*, but I'm not pregnant, either."

"Neither was I, last summer."

Eliza knew Jane was so happy expecting a child that she was willing to endure any discomfort. She also knew Levy and Jane earned the bulk of their year's income during the busy summer months when they sold whatever they could at the weekly farmers market. "Things may change next summer, when you try to handle the same workload but with a baby," she warned.

"*Ja*, I know you're right." Jane lifted the toddler onto her lap. "Levy and I have discussed what to do if I can't keep up with the same amount of work. We might start selling crafts and baked goods for others in exchange for some of the profit, rather than making or growing everything ourselves."

"That's a *gut* idea. Kind of like what your aunt and uncle do with their store—they sell what others make."

"Exactly." Jane focused on Eliza's face. "Now let's change the subject. What's wrong?"

Startled, Eliza looked up at her sister-in-law. "What do you mean?"

"I mean, you look like a thundercloud is resting on your head. Are you upset about something?"

Eliza blessed Jane's perception. "Just annoyed, I guess."

"Why?"

"I heard something a few minutes ago. Josiah and one of his crew members were talking upstairs. I admit I eavesdropped." She related the conversation she'd overheard. "I suspect I'm to blame for how he feels about dating all these women," she concluded, "and also why his mother is pushing him to marry someone, anyone. It's like I'm caught in the middle without even knowing about it. And suddenly it made me angry. I've been very careful to live by the *Ordnung* even though I'm not baptized. I've promised myself to be guided by *Gott* at every step. So why should I feel guilty over what Josiah is feeling?" Her hands clenched.

"That's easy. You shouldn't."

"I know. It just makes me mad that it bothers me. I wish I could tell him what I think, but I don't even know what to say when I see him. I get tongue-tied." She snorted. "Maybe I should write him a letter."

"Maybe don't write a letter, but write a script," suggested Jane. She handed Mercy back and stood up to pour the tea from the boiling kettle.

"A script?" Eliza stared at her sister-in-law.

"*Ja*, sure. That way you can make sure you're saying exactly what you want to say, without getting tongue-tied. Tell him just what you told me—that you're not the guilty party here, and give your blessing for him to court whomever he wants, or whatever else you want to convey. Sometimes it's best to just clear the air." She set mugs of tea on the table.

"That's a *gut* idea," admitted Eliza. Her mind buzzed with what she could tell Josiah if she could just manage to get some clarity. She leaned over and kissed her sister-in-law on the cheek. "The best thing Levy ever did was marry you. I'm so glad you're my sister."

Jane smiled. "Let me get you some paper and a pen. We can go through some thoughts you want to tell him, and then you can spend some time memorizing the points you want to make."

"Let me put Mercy down for a nap. It looks like she's about to drop off anyway." The baby's eyes were drooping.

A few minutes later, having settled the toddler in her crib, Eliza sat back down in the kitchen with a sheet of paper in front of her. "Okay, let's brainstorm."

"What are you most annoyed about this situation?" began Jane.

"That I'm somehow caught in the middle without knowing why."

"*Gut*. Write that down."

Eliza did. "Also, that I promised *Gott* not to interfere with his romantic life." She wrote some more.

"And what about his mother?" asked Jane. "How you don't know why she's playing matchmaker and pressuring Josiah to marry, but it's none of your business and you have no intention of causing a rift in his family?"

"Ja, gut." Eliza's pen flew. "And also, I want the best for him, so it's best if he marries someone without my complicated past."

"Are you sure you want to include that?" inquired Jane. "The past is past."

"Ja, but the past has repercussions." Eliza mimicked rocking a baby. "Marrying Bill was a big mistake, and if *Gott* hadn't taken him when he did, I'd be miserable right now. And so would Mercy."

"And I suppose if you hadn't left the community in the first place, none of the complications would have happened," admitted Jane. "So *ja*, include that if you want."

"I will. Besides, it's something I feel strongly about. As much as I wish I could turn back the clock, I can't. In other words, I wouldn't wish me on anyone." Tears prickled her eyes.

Jane reached out and patted Eliza's hand for a moment. "Oh, Eliza, don't think less of yourself than *Gott* does. Don't despair. *Gott* has a way of making things work out. Last summer I cried my eyes out over Levy. I was convinced he couldn't see past my plainness to the person I was underneath. My aunt Catherine had to slap me upside the head once or twice to get me out of my self-pity."

"I can't believe you ever thought you were plain."

"It doesn't matter now. Your brother sees what I look like inside, not outside. I never thought it was possible for me to be as happy as I am right now. So, just like Aunt Catherine helped me get my head clear, maybe I need to do the same with you."

Eliza smiled, though her eyes still prickled. "No need. I've acknowledged my sins and asked for *Gott*'s forgiveness. My path is clear. It won't be easy, but it's clear." She rose. "I'm going to go compose this into something coherent. Do you want to read it over before I talk to Josiah?"

"Not unless you want me to. It's yours and should come from the heart."

Eliza nodded. "I'll have to find a time when he's by himself."

"He walks home by himself. Maybe you could 'accidentally' cross his path. I can watch Mercy while you talk to him."

"Ja, danke."

Throughout Mercy's nap, Eliza ignored her sewing and worked on the script. She wrote things down, crossed things out, added things, changed things…all in an effort to make sure her thoughts were as clear and precise as possible. She made bullet points on the script and memorized them.

She started by recapping the flawed adolescent logic that led her to leave her Amish community, and how—with the selfishness of youth—she didn't realize the impact her departure would have on her brother, her friends or on him, Josiah. She outlined briefly the regrettable episode of her hasty marriage to Bill, and the circumstances under which he died. She confessed her guilt for the relief she felt to be free of an unfortunate marriage. She related the desperation she felt when she sent her baby to her brother. And she told the story of the pastor and his wife who paid for her trip back, and her promise to pay that favor forward one day.

She reiterated her regret in leaving him behind when she left the community, but hoped he would find another young woman who didn't carry the burden of a complicated past. She promised never to do anything that would interfere with his relationship with anyone.

Eliza laid down her pen and leaned back in the chair, drained. Drained, but more at peace. Confession was good for the soul, she knew, and she felt better. Lighter. It was necessary to clarify her feelings for Josiah—her feelings and her position—so no blame could be laid at her feet about how she conducted herself.

She read over the notes once more, then nodded her head. She'd made her position clear and certain.

Now all it would take was for Josiah to respect that position. But that was his choice, not hers.

Josiah slipped his hammer into the loop on his tool belt and watched as his crew headed home for the evening.

"Tomorrow we'll start on the siding," he told Levy. "Work is progressing well. You'll have lots of room for the *boppli* that's coming, as well as any more." He paused and scanned the sky. "The weather has been so *gut* this far, we haven't had to take any rain days. But if the past is anything to go by, we can expect at least one good thunderstorm this month. I want to make sure to get the new roofing up as soon as possible."

Levy removed his straw hat and wiped sweat from his forehead with a handkerchief. "You're a *gut* carpenter, Josiah. I'm glad we hired you." He reached over to shake Josiah's hand. "See you tomorrow."

"Ja." Josiah moved through the unfinished downstairs, removed his tool belt and dropped it in a corner with the rest of the tools he kept at the work site. He wiped his face with a ban-

danna, replaced his hat and walked out of the house toward home.

Passing a thicket of bushes under some large shady trees, he heard his name. "Josiah?"

"Ja?" He paused.

To his surprise, Eliza stepped out of the bushes. His heart thumped at the sight. She pleated the edge of her apron in a gesture that caught his eye. When she saw him watching, she dropped the cloth, straightened her shoulders and said, "I wanted to talk to you."

Against all reason, he felt a wild shaft of hope run through him. If she'd gone to the trouble of waiting in a clump of bushes for him, it must be important.

He kept his face neutral. "About what?"

"I—I have a confession to make. I overheard part of your conversation earlier today with one of your workmen. The conversation where you were discussing how your mother is playing matchmaker."

"Oh." Embarrassment flared. What a thing for her to hear. "What about it?" He heard the faint note of hostility in his own voice.

Her cheeks flushed and she raised her chin. "I wanted to clear the air," she said. "We've avoided each other ever since I came home, so I've never told you why I left."

"Why you abandoned me, you mean," he spat.

He drew a ragged breath and closed his eyes. "I'm sorry, that was uncalled for."

"No, it wasn't. I *did* abandon you. I abandoned my brother. I—I even abandoned *Gott*. Will you listen to me if I explain it?"

"*Ja*, sure." He gestured toward the trunk of the tree, "These bushes will give us privacy. I will listen, Eliza."

She turned and sat on the ground, her legs tucked to the side. He lowered himself with his back against the trunk.

And she talked. Blurted, almost, with a stiffness he suspected was rehearsed to some extent. She told him why she left as a teen, briefly outlined her disastrous marriage and then rapid widowhood, her desperate logic to send Mercy to her brother to raise. She told about the kindly pastor and his wife who rescued her from despair and returned her to her community.

"And this is why I want you to take your mother's advice and marry someone, anyone, who isn't me," she concluded. She clasped her hands in her lap. "I've made such a mess of my life."

He remained silent through her confession, his own thoughts twisted and chaotic. Finally he said, "Eliza, let me ask you something. I still don't understand why you wanted to leave. What caused you to leave the church and the community? It's not uncommon for young men to go away. But less common for young women."

"I don't know. Yes, I do," she immediately contradicted. "I—I thought I knew better. I fought against the restrictions of the *Ordnung* because I didn't understand the peace of mind it represents. I came back because I realized I was wrong. It's one of the reasons I'm committed to living as pure a life as possible." She gestured toward the bushes shielding them from sight. "Even to the point of talking with you only in secret."

He nodded, better understanding the depths of despair she'd experienced, the youthful rebellion gone astray when it crashed into the harsh reality of bad choices and a bad man. And he recoiled further from the *Englisch* world that had lured her away from the secure community in which she'd grown up.

At his silence, a look of frustration crossed her face. "Well?" she demanded. "Aren't you going to say anything?"

"What can I say?" he replied, trying to keep a note of judgment out of his voice. "You're abandoning me again."

She gasped. "What?"

"What I get out of this, Eliza, is you're so focused on yourself, you have no room to consider the feelings of anyone else." He rose to his feet and dusted off the seat of his pants. "You're so convinced you're damaged goods that you refuse to see what's in front of you."

She scrambled to her feet and confronted him, arms akimbo. Her eyes snapped and pink tinged her cheeks. "I simply wanted to make it clear that I'm not waiting in the wings for you in any way. I'm determined to avoid gossip from people waiting to pounce on any mistake I make. Didn't you hear me? I'm promising you I won't do anything to interfere with your romantic prospects, whatever they may be."

"Don't you care about what I think?" he demanded. "What I want?"

"Maybe you should ask your mother," she snapped. "For once your mother and I agree. I'm not the right woman for you, and that's all there is to it."

"As you say." He didn't feel like arguing, and he tried not to admire how spirited she looked when angry. "I spent a lot of time being furious with you, Eliza. Always I wondered if there was something I'd done to chase you away. I see there wasn't. But now that you're back, there are just as many obstacles in the way. Maybe my mother's right. Maybe you're right. There are plenty of other fish in the sea."

"No doubt." She stood rigid, her chin up. "And no doubt Ruby will help you hook the best one. I'd even be willing to guide you toward someone more suitable. Goodbye, Josiah." She spun on her heel and stalked away.

He stared after her, ashamed of himself. He hadn't meant to blurt out some of the things he'd said. He'd certainly not meant to hurt her.

Her back was rigid, her hands clenched. He felt like he was watching his future stalk away. He looked ahead, down the long path of his future, and didn't like what he saw. It made him want to run, bolt, flee from the stifling expectations being laid before him.

He remembered what Eliza had said about the twisted teenage logic behind her excursion into the *Englisch* world, and suddenly—for the first time—he understood what caused her to run. She didn't want to fulfill the stifling expectations of young women. She wanted more.

Well, she got more, all right—and having tasted it, she chose to return to her roots. Not just return, but embrace everything from which she had fled.

But he, himself, who had never before felt the urge to leave his community, now experienced a desire to simply run away from his problems. How was he different from Eliza? He was older, more mature than she was when she left. But he had the same urge to kick back at the prospects expected of him, and metaphorically run away.

"You *dummkopf*," he muttered. He realized at some level he *was* hoping Eliza was waiting in the wings for him. In fact, a great deal of his annoyance with his mother's perpetual match-making on his behalf stemmed from that hope.

He stared at the ground, mentally kicking himself, remembering how he felt when Eliza first left the community. He was tormented by why she left and what she might be facing in the *Englisch* world. But now—how was he treating her since she'd come back? Was he acting like a forgiving man? No.

Josiah slumped against the tree trunk and tried to think. His avenues seemed to be closing. His mother continued to push eligible women into his path, women he tried to let down gently because he simply wasn't interested.

And Eliza, by her own promise, was off-limits to him. Up until now, he hadn't realized just how much he secretly hoped she would fall into his arms in a gesture of undying love and devotion, and thus rescue him from the expectation that he would court and marry someone else.

One thing was certain: he would not allow his mother to interfere in his love life again. He was a grown man and needed to make up his mind about what he wanted to do, how he wanted his future to unfold.

And how should he treat Eliza? He couldn't

be angry with her. Nor did she deserve to be snubbed or ignored. He should treat her as any Christian man should treat her—with politeness, respect, friendliness. But, he vowed to himself, never would he cross the line into any behavior that would make her uncomfortable.

Thus resolved, he headed home.

Chapter Six

Eliza didn't sleep well that night. She tossed and turned. In her heart she knew she'd done the right thing, and she labored to bring her rebellious spirit into submission.

And rebellion, it seemed, was part of her nature. That's what sent her fleeing the community when she was younger, wasn't it? She thought she had conquered her mutinous personality after what she went through in the *Englisch* world. And now, fearing she was irrevocably stuck on Josiah, she prayed she wouldn't go down that same dangerous path again.

Josiah's behavior was only to be expected, but it didn't make her future any easier. Once again, Eliza wondered if she'd done the right thing, coming home. It wasn't too late to change. It wasn't baptized; she was free to leave and rejoin the *Englisch* world. Could she?

But were her romantic complications reason enough to turn her back on Levy and Jane? Was it fair to deprive Mercy of her family, and the community support every Amish child grew up with? Or was she, as Josiah had accused, thinking only of herself?

She was heavy-eyed and depressed when she dragged herself out of bed the next morning. She dreaded seeing Josiah during the course of his workday, wondering what he would say or how he would react.

But he said nothing. Not that day, nor the next, nor the next. He didn't speak to her, he hardly looked at her, and he certainly didn't seek her out. Instead he concentrated on his work, creating the home expansion, consulting Levy or Jane when necessary, but otherwise involved in hammering and sawing.

If she had secretly hoped her conversation would soften him, would make him fall into her arms in a gesture of undying love and devotion, she was wrong. Instead, it seemed he was angry with her. And who could blame him?

So she sewed. She sewed furiously. She sewed more dolls than she could possibly imagine she could sew. She poured heart and soul into her work, which left her room only for lavishing attention on Mercy.

On Friday, Josiah finally broke his silence.

Eliza carried a large box with new dolls outside, ready to pack it into the wagon for the next day's farmers market. Unfortunately she didn't see the tree root that sent her—and the box of dolls—sprawling.

She heard an exclamation, and a moment later Josiah helped her to her feet. "Are you all right?"

"*Ja*, except for my dignity." She dusted off her apron. "*Danke.*" She kept her voice neutral and tried not to convey how fast her heart started beating from his touch.

He crouched down and started collecting the dolls that had spilled from the box. "These are for the farmers market tomorrow?"

"*Ja.* This is just one of the boxes. I have two more in the house, as well as a batch for the Troyers' store. Catherine and Peter sell some for me, too."

"They're nice." He paused to examine the traditional faceless figure. "As nice as I've ever seen."

"*Danke.*" Her voice held a startled note. His praise, not to mention the fact that he didn't simply go away after assisting her up, surprised her. Was he as angry as she'd imagined? Whatever his mindset, it was none of her business. Her only business was to control her behavior and keep the conversation impersonal.

"Are they selling that well?" he asked.

"*Ja.* They've been selling so well it's hard to keep up."

"Wow. That's *gut.*"

She looked down at the doll in her hands. "I like making toys for young children that aren't like the ones I saw in the *Englisch* world."

"What were those like?"

"Very garish. Plastic, bright colors, often based on television characters. I didn't want any of that for Mercy, just a Plain doll and simple toys. I didn't realize how much interest other *Englisch* mothers had in simple toys, as well."

"Maybe they're also tired of garish, plastic toys." Josiah tucked the doll back into the box and took a step back. "It sounds like you have a nice little business."

"I like making them." Eliza smoothed down a tiny dress, and her voice grew animated. "I've started ordering sewing materials wholesale through the Troyers' store. The money I bring in helps with the household income, too. Levy and Jane have been so *gut* to me, so I'm glad to be helping out."

"Your eyes are sparkling," he observed. A smile played across his face.

She jerked her head up and immediately blanked her expression. Was he flirting? Whatever hidden hurt feelings she carried—or for that matter, he harbored—she would not allow them to come to the surface. "We were talking about the dolls," she reminded him.

"*Ja*, sure. The dolls." He looked down at the box of toys. "But I understand your enthusiasm. I admire how you're taking your worldly experience and using it to the good. It's like you're countering the bad examples you witnessed. There's something to be said for that, Eliza."

"*Danke.*" She felt wary of his praise. He was a forbidden fruit for her, and she didn't want to follow Eve's example and give in to temptation. In their own world, the repercussions could be just as far-reaching. "Well, I'll just take these to the barn. That's where Levy stacks the things he brings to the farmers market."

"I'll carry it." He hoisted the box into his arms and walked toward the outbuilding.

Eliza trotted behind him, feeling agitated. She didn't want their interaction seen—or misinterpreted—by anyone. She still felt like her reputation was at stake, and that she was walking a fine line of respectability.

In the barn, Levy stacked crates of tomatoes and corn. He turned and elevated his eyebrows when he saw Josiah holding the box.

"Where do you want this?" asked Josiah.

"What is it?"

Eliza piped up. "Dolls."

Patrice Lewis 99

"Right there." Levy pointed.

Josiah put the box where indicated, touched his hat brim, nodded at Eliza and left the barn.

"What was that all about?" Levy pushed back his hat brim and scratched his head. She saw amusement on his face.

"I tripped while carrying the box." Eliza felt her face flush and hoped the burning color wasn't obvious in the shadowy barn. "Josiah helped me up and then carried the box in here."

"Is that all?" The amusement blossomed into a grin.

She glared. "*Ja*, that's all. Don't create something that isn't there, Levy."

"I wouldn't dream of it." He turned back to stacking crates of vegetables. "How many more boxes of dolls do you have?"

"Two more. I'll bring them out." She spun around and walked away.

"Don't trip!" her brother called after her.

Eliza's annoyance at her brother's teasing became tempered by a smile. Even in the midst of the summer pressure of work, Levy was in much better humor than he used to be. She remembered him as being grim and stern when she was younger, probably from the pressure of raising a rebellious sister after their parents died. She knew she hurt him badly when she left the community, one of her many regrets. But now he was happier. Calmer.

Reentering the kitchen, Eliza saw the reason for her brother's sunnier disposition—his wife. Jane was not, Eliza admitted, a pretty woman, and right now looked plainer than usual. Her face was sweaty, her glasses kept inching down her nose, but she had the same happy inner glow about her as Levy did. They were made for one another. There were times Eliza envied them their happiness.

Jane took fresh bread from the oven and slid the hot loaf pans onto cooling racks. The bread and other baked goods were for tomorrow's sales at the farmers market. Mercy sat in her high chair, gumming a soft roll.

"Got your sewing all done?" Jane asked.

"*Ja.* I have two more boxes of dolls to bring out. That's three boxes total, as well as another two boxes to bring to your aunt and uncle's store." Eliza dropped onto a kitchen chair. "*Ach,* what a busy week it's been."

"And probably a fairly emotional one, too." Jane wiped a trickle of sweat off her face with the corner of her apron. "Has Josiah said anything further from your conversation?" Jane knew about the confrontation.

"No," replied Eliza. "None. In fact, Josiah

spent the last few days completely avoiding and ignoring me, until just a few minutes ago."

"What happened a few minutes ago?"

"I tripped while carrying a box of dolls. He came over to help me up, then carried the box into the barn for me."

"That was a courteous thing to do." Jane's eyebrows rose. "Was there more to it than that?"

"I don't know." Eliza flapped a hand in agitation. "He asked me about my sewing business, complimented the quality of the dolls, and then…then… And then he said my eyes were sparkling." She felt herself blush again.

"I see." Jane sat down opposite the table. She sighed. "That doesn't sound like something a man would say unless he was…"

"Flirting." Eliza nearly spat the word. "And it messed me up inside again. I thought I'd made my position perfectly clear, then he goes and says something like that."

Jane shook her head. "Nothing is ever easy in this life, is it? Especially in matters of the heart."

"I'm trying to control my heart. It's just not as easy as I thought." A movement outside caught her eye through the window. She nodded toward what she saw. "See? Case in point."

Jane twisted in her seat and said nothing as she watched Jodie—the pretty young woman

Josiah had courted for a while—walk across the lawn, picnic basket in hand, straight toward Josiah.

"How can I compete with that?" murmured Eliza.

It was with mild annoyance that Josiah watched Jodie pick her way amid the construction debris, picnic basket in hand, toward him. Of all the women his mother had set him up with, Jodie was the hardest to shake. She seemed to think she could win him over by her sweetness and thoughtful actions, such as a picnic lunch. But Josiah was still struggling after his short conversation with Eliza five minutes before. The fact that the brief, neutral chat unsettled him so much made him mad at himself.

He compensated by putting on his best smile as he greeted her. "Beautiful day, *ja*?"

"*Ja*. I thought you might like some lunch. I made some of those meat pasties I know you like."

"Let's break for now," Josiah told his crew. He followed Jodie toward a large maple tree, trying to think of ways to be polite without encouraging her.

The young woman removed a thin quilt from the basket, shook it out and settled it on the ground. Josiah sat down as she removed boxes and tins of delicious homemade goodies.

"You must spend all morning working on making a lunch like this," he commented.

"A bit, *ja*. I like making *gut* meals." She smiled at him, her blue eyes glinting in the dapples of sun through the branches.

He joined her in a silent blessing over the food, then bit into a meat pasty. "What have you been doing this morning? Besides packing such a wonderful picnic lunch?"

He tried to act interested as Jodie chattered about helping a neighbor who'd just had a baby, how it was nice to be helpful around the house as the new mother adjusted to infant care.

"You're a *gut* woman, Jodie," he said, impressed. "I know Anna Miller thinks so, too, as she gets used to her new baby."

Silence lapsed. Jodie ate some of the macaroni salad she'd brought. Josiah nibbled on a biscuit. He sighed inside and decided to be blunt. "Jodie, you don't have to do this, you know." He gestured at the picnic spread.

"Don't you like good food?" She looked hurt.

"Of course I like good food. I've seldom had better. You're very talented. But Jodie… It's not going to work." He felt like a louse at the expression on her face.

"I see." Jodie stared at the items spread out on the quilt. "I—I guess I'll get going, then."

"*Vielen Dank* for lunch. It was delicious."

Silently Jodie repacked the basket, gave him a long, lingering look and walked away.

Josiah watched her leave. Jodie was a good woman. All the women he'd dated were good women. Why couldn't he find it in him to enjoy their company?

A thought struck him. While he was busy deciding all the docile, charming young women his mother put in his path wouldn't make him happy, he wondered at the reverse. Could he make a woman happy? Would he be a good husband?

A movement caught his eye. He glimpsed Eliza through the kitchen window, moving back and forth at some task. Jane and Levy bustled about getting ready for the morrow's farmers market.

How could he prefer the fiery and complicated woman in the house to the placid woman who had just walked away? As he started back at work, he was also eaten up with guilt because he knew the answer.

"If you can spare me, I'm going to take this order of dolls to your uncle's store," Eliza announced to Jane.

Her sister-in-law paused in her work. "*Ja.* There's not a lot you can do here at the moment, since you've already packed up what you're selling tomorrow at the market. But you'll have to take Mercy with you, since I'm so busy here."

"Of course." Eliza felt some guilt. Her desire to deliver the order of dolls to the Troyers' store had more to do with escaping the sight of Josiah than a burning need to deliver the dolls right away. Friday was the busiest day for her brother and sister-in-law as they prepared for the Saturday market, but Eliza also knew she would be more in the way of their efficient routine by offering to help.

"You can take the wagon if you like," added Jane. "That will help with the boxes."

"*Ja, danke.* Don't worry, I'll take care of things."

Eliza slipped Mercy into the sling she usually used while carrying the baby, then pulled the child's hand wagon from the barn and parked it in the front of the house. She entered the home and placed the baby inside the barricaded sewing area. "Stay here a moment, *liebling,*" she told the toddler. "*Mamm* will be right back."

Eliza moved swiftly to load the boxes of dolls into the wagon, but Mercy fussed and cried because she wanted to follow. "Now, now," crooned Eliza, lifting her child up and settling her in the sling. "Let's go for a little walk, shall we?"

She left the house, seized the handle of the wagon and started on the half-mile trip to the Troyers' store. Mercy immediately settled into bright-eyed watchfulness.

Eliza loved the feel of the child riding her hip, secure in the fabric sling against her body. She knew babies developed better with close body contact, and because Mercy was bottle-fed, the extra closeness was important for her development. Certainly she was, on the whole, a happy and alert child.

Soon enough she approached the store and pulled the wagon up the ramp built at one end of the building's wide wooden porch. She left the wagon outside. As she pushed open the door, a bell tinkled overhead. The store had a fair number of people inside, talking and chattering in English as they examined the goods on display.

Catherine Troyer looked up from behind the counter. "*Guder nammidaag*, Eliza. Have you brought another shipment of dolls?"

"*Guder nammidaag. Ja*, I have two boxes outside."

"Here, I'll take the *liebling* if you want to bring them inside." She held out her arms.

Eliza slipped Mercy out of the sling and

handed her to the grandmotherly woman, who started crooning at the child. Eliza made two trips and brought in the boxes of dolls.

"They're selling well," said Catherine. She gestured around the store. "Lots of tourists this summer, and it seems they all want dolls. If you want to bring the boxes over to that corner, I'll get them inventoried."

Eliza lugged one of the boxes to the spot Catherine had indicated. As she hoisted the second, she heard a voice say, "Whoa! Let me help you with that!" A burly *Englisch* man with a friendly face took the box from her arms. "Where do you want it?"

"Over there, please." She pointed.

He walked across the store and deposited the box on the floor where indicated. Then he brushed off his hands and cocked an eyebrow. "There you go."

"*Danke.* That was very kind."

"What's in these?" He pointed to the boxes.

"Dolls. I make them for selling here at this store." She opened a flap and pulled out a sample.

"Very nice." He looked over the doll, then looked up at her. "May I buy you a cup of coffee? I'd like to hear more about them."

She froze. The man's fast move shocked her, especially since for all he knew she was married. As her face warmed, she glanced quickly around to see if anyone from the community was watching, and was chagrined to notice an Amish woman with her husband grimacing at the exchange. Plastering a smile on her face, she lied, saying very loudly, "No, but thank you. My husband is waiting for me outside."

"Ah. I see. Well, good luck with the doll sales." He handed her back the cloth figure and walked out of the store.

She turned to watch him leave, and intercepted Catherine's amused gaze.

"Whew." Eliza walked over to take Mercy back. "That was interesting."

"It happens." The older woman's eyes crinkled. "Even to me." Catherine spoke in German.

Eliza was shocked. "*Englisch* men ask you out?"

"*Ja*, once in a while. Even at my age. I think sometimes a *kapp* comes across as a challenge." She touched her head covering.

"Well, I certainly wasn't interested."

"Which leads to a question. Is there anyone who *does* interest you?"

She kept her voice light. "Sure, but he's off-limits, remember? And right now I'm too busy repairing my reputation. Becoming interested in anyone would just fuel future gossip. Why risk it?"

"I guess." Catherine switched to speaking English. "I'll be happy to ring that up for you…" she told a pleasant-faced matron.

While Catherine waited upon the customer, Eliza browsed the store. She stopped at a display of small baby quilts, noticing the fine stitching and colorful patterns. A small tag on each quilt indicated the maker, none other than Ruby.

"She does excellent work, doesn't she?" Catherine joined her in looking at the display.

"*Ja.* I don't think I've seen better." Eliza sighed.

"Is it awkward to have Josiah working on Levy's house expansion?"

"Sometimes. We avoid each other." She fiddled with a corner of a quilt. "But it's okay. I made a promise to *Gott* that it wouldn't be a problem."

"Promises are *gut* and I'm glad you intend to keep them," observed Catherine, "but it doesn't always change what the heart feels."

"Perhaps not, but what matters isn't how I feel, it's how I behave." She lifted her gaze to see Catherine watching her with so much compassion, she felt her eyes prickle. "And that's what I've promised to do. I have a lot of ground to make up, a lot of mistakes to atone for. Expressing interest in a man who I hurt badly, and whose mother doesn't like me, isn't how to get there."

Catherine nodded. "Those are wise words, child. But don't despair. *Gott* has a way of making things work out. Perhaps someone you haven't noticed has been noticing you."

"I can't imagine why. I'm not worth noticing." She gave a small, bitter laugh. "Except perhaps to *Englischers* for whom a *kapp* is a challenge."

Chapter Seven

❧

"They all sold," announced Jane late on Saturday after returning from the farmers market. "Every last doll."

"Really!" Eliza grinned. "That's *gut*!"

"You should come with us some time. That man was back who wants to talk to you. He says he's a wholesaler who might want to carry your dolls."

"Ach." Eliza rubbed her chin. "I just don't know if I can make dolls any faster than I am now, though. But maybe I'll take your place at the farmers market next week and see if he's there. It would be interesting to talk to him."

"Have you thought about hiring someone to help you sew?"

"No, but that's an idea. I would have to be selling enough to be able to pay for the work and still earn money."

Jane changed the subject. "Levy says he wants to go into town next week. He wants to bring me along, too, as a sort of day off for both of us, a chance to get away from the constant work. So if you have anything you want us to pick up, just let me know."

Grand Creek was a tiny town, and once in a while Levy needed to do some shopping in the nearby city of Lafayette.

"Ja, danke," replied Eliza. "I'll think about it."

All week long, Eliza watched as Levy and Jane worked even longer hours, so they could plan for a day off to take their trip into town. They chose Thursday as their mini-vacation.

"Maybe I should go instead of you," she told them at breakfast on Thursday morning over the din of hammers from the work crew. "I can run errands for you. Your summers are so busy that even taking one day off to go to town is almost too much."

"Actually, I'm looking forward to it." Jane broke a muffin into small pieces for Mercy, perched in her high chair. "It's nice to get away from the work routine. Levy even promised to buy me lunch." She winked at her husband.

Eliza laughed. Her brother and sister-in-law's transparent happiness shone through everything, even though she knew they were both bone-weary from the heavy workload. "Well, have fun. I intend to stay home and finish this week's production run of dolls. Catherine told me they were selling well in the store, too."

"Will you be able to keep up?" Levy speared a sausage.

"I think so, *ja*. This week I figured out a technique to make the doll clothes faster than I did before, and that was always the part that slowed me down the most." She reached over and wiped some crumbs off her daughter's face. "I'm still learning my trade, you might say, and this new system lets me make more dolls in less time, so we'll see what happens."

"That's *gut*," approved Levy. He glanced at the clock. "We should get going," he told Jane. "I noticed clouds building up and would rather get to town and back before any rain moves in."

"*Ja*, sure, I'm ready." Jane pushed back her chair and rose to her feet.

With Mercy in her arms, Eliza watched the horse and buggy clip-clop away a few moments later. The house seemed quiet after her brother and sister-in-law left, even though the work crew continued to clatter and hammer on the house extension. After putting Mercy down for her morning nap, Eliza tackled her own workload.

It wasn't until an hour and a half later that she

raised her head from her sewing upon hearing Mercy's cries. She hurried to find her daughter standing in her crib, fretful after waking up from her nap. "*Ach, liebling, Mamm*'s here," she murmured, picking up the baby and snuggling her. "Would you like a bottle?"

She went into the kitchen, prepared a bottle of formula, and settled into the rocking chair with her. The toddler ate solid foods mostly now, but enjoyed the comforting routine of rocking and nursing when she woke up.

She hardly paid attention to the rising wind and darkening clouds outside until she heard Josiah call to his men, "Pack it in, boys!" The hammers went still, and he continued, "Looks like we're in for a storm cell. Can't work in these conditions. We'll pick up tomorrow."

In some alarm, she rose from the rocking chair, clutching the baby. She went through the door into the new house extension and saw the men putting away their tools. "Is it a tornado?" she cried.

Josiah shook his head. "I don't think so, just a fast-moving thunderstorm. Don't worry, Eliza."

She nodded and retreated from the construction zone. Then she tucked Mercy into the sling and went outside to batten down the hatches— bringing in the horses and cows from their fields, making sure the barn doors were secured, rescuing some baskets of produce Levy had left in the shade of the maple tree in the backyard. The clouds overhead were dark and ominous, and gusts of wind flapped her skirt and whipped tree branches. She looked at the verdant garden and fields and bit her lip. These plots were a huge part of her brother's livelihood. "Please, *Gott*, don't let the storm damage them too much…"

Then as the wind picked up harder and the rain started lashing, she fled into the house. She put Mercy down on the floor near her sewing machine in the barricaded work area, which had become a de facto playpen for the child. Thunder and lightning flashed and crashed around them. Eliza went to stand near the bank of windows overlooking the backyard, and watched the rising storm. She wished Levy and Jane were back home and safe.

A mighty gust shook the house and bent the maple tree outside. Eliza gasped as a huge branch tore off the tree with a giant *crack*. The branch crashed into the unfinished construction area of the house expansion, collapsing some of the studs and roofing. Then, to her horror, the massive branch bounced, rolled and hit the side of the house where she stood watching through the window. The casement shattered, showering her with glass and splinters of wood.

She screamed, then froze. The branch settled, half in the house and half out, surrounded by pieces of glass and cracked wood. She was afraid to move amid the shattered glass all around her along with the debris from the broken wall. She felt something warm on her face and lifted her hand to touch it. Blood. She was covered in glass.

Mercy wailed in fear from her place on the other side of the room. She needed help. Blinking through blood, Eliza hoped the baby was safe, just frightened. Covered in glass shards and torn by branches, she knew she couldn't pick up her baby without terrifying her...

She heard an exclamation and looked up to see Josiah, a scrape on his forehead but otherwise unhurt. He dashed in from the construction zone. "Eliza, are you okay?"

"Mercy. Take care of Mercy..." Her teeth chattered as adrenaline flooded her system.

"Let me get you out of there."

"No! I'm covered with glass. Take care of Mercy."

"Can you walk?" Fear creased his face.

"Yes." She began to pick her way through the debris from the window, glass crunching under her shoes. "Please, take care of Mercy." Her baby's wails pierced her anew.

Josiah turned and strode over to the barricade, and lifted the toddler into his arms. "There, there, *liebling*," he crooned, stroking her hair. He pulled a handkerchief out of his pocket and mopped the child's tears.

Eliza stepped away from the zone of debris. She shook her clothing, hearing tinkles of glass fall around her.

Josiah bit his lip. "Every instinct tells me to help you."

"You can't." She swiped her face and her hand came away covered with more blood, startling amounts of blood. Oddly there wasn't much pain, but there was so much blood. "You can't pull the glass off me."

"Did the branch land on you?"

"No, it just broke the window. I happened to be standing close enough to get covered…"

Another flash of lightning lit his face, and a crack of thunder boomed. Mercy renewed her wails.

"Josiah, I need you to keep Mercy while I change clothes. I can't hold her while I'm wearing this in case she gets cut. Can you do that?"

"*Ja*, sure." His face was still a study in concern. "But if you look at yourself in the mirror, don't be too shocked. You look pretty bad."

"Do I?" She looked at the blood on her hands. Her brain felt thick and stupid. "*Ja*, I have to get cleaned up…"

Another gust of wind shook the house, but the storm cell seemed to be passing. Blinking through the stickiness on her face, Eliza went upstairs to her bedroom. She removed her clothes and piled them in a corner, knowing she'd have to examine them carefully for bits of glass. She donned clean clothes, then went into the bathroom to wash her face and hands.

She gasped when she saw herself in the mirror. Josiah was right. She looked bad. Nicks and scrapes and cuts adorned her face. She knew facial cuts bled heavily even when they weren't deep, and she didn't feel badly hurt. But yes, she looked terrible.

Thankfully, she didn't see any splinters of glass to remove, so she wet a cloth and washed her face, wincing as the cuts stung. But after she'd tidied her hair and affixed a clean *kapp*, she looked better.

By now, Mercy's cries had quieted, and so did Eliza's worry. She descended the stairs and entered the living room to find Josiah holding the baby in the rocking chair. Mercy leaned her head against Josiah's chest in a trusting posture that brought tears to Eliza's eyes. The baby looked half-asleep.

Josiah's head jerked up when she entered. "Are you okay?"

"*Ja.* Just shaken up. You're right, I looked pretty bad, but I'm not much hurt."

He blew out a breath. "I was scared to death when I saw you standing there covered in blood."

"*Mamm...*" Mercy raised her head and held out her arms to Eliza.

"Sit here." Josiah rose and handed her the baby.

Eliza sat down and cuddled Mercy in her lap, rocking the child, who seemed calmer.

"Where do you keep the medical supplies?" asked Josiah.

"Why?"

"Because I'm worried about those cuts on your arms and face."

"In the bathroom cabinet." She jerked her head toward the hallway.

Josiah departed and returned a few moments later with cotton balls, bacitracin ointment and a box of bandages. He dragged over a chair and sat nearby.

"Don't move," he ordered. He swabbed the cotton ball with the ointment and started applying it to her wounds on her face—cheeks, forehead, chin. Even her neck was sliced.

Eliza bit her lip and kept her eyes lowered. His actions were intimate and personal. Yet there was no question her skin felt better wherever he dabbed the ointment.

"Let me see your arm." He plucked up a fresh cotton ball.

Clutching Mercy in one arm, she held out the other. Josiah clucked over one gash. "I hope this won't need stitches. Does it hurt much?"

"Oddly, no. I feel a little dazed, but nothing really hurts."

"We'll see how you feel tomorrow." He cleaned the deepest cut, then bandaged it. "Now let me see your other arm."

Eliza complied, but couldn't help a mild protest. "You don't have to do this."

"It makes me feel less helpless. I don't think I've ever been as scared as when I saw you there covered in blood and glass shards." He finished cleaning her cuts. "There. Does it feel better?"

"Ja." She felt herself blush. *"Danke."*

He nodded, got up to put the medical supplies on a table, then set his chair back to a more respectful distance.

Anxious to divert her attention from his tender ministrations, Eliza touched Mercy's hair. "You have a *gut* touch with babies. Thank you for taking care of her."

"She's a sweetheart. And I think she would have responded to anyone, just because she was so scared. As I was," he added.

"But you got hurt, too." She gestured toward the scrape on his forehead. "I'm surprised you're still here."

"I was just putting some tools away before I went home. I think *Gott* had me linger so I could offer help when that tree branch came down."

Eliza looked over the chaotic living room. "Levy and Jane are going to be horrified when they see the damage."

"*Ach*, it looks bad, but I can fix it up. I even have some extra windows I can use to replace these. In the meantime, I will cover them with something before I go."

"You're a *gut* man, Josiah." Eliza leaned her head back and sighed. *"Danke."* Despite the pounding rain outside, she felt cozy and warm with him here to help her. The wind had eased, so the room was safe from the damp for now.

"Eliza…about our conversation the other day…"

She shrank into wariness and looked at him. *"Ja?"*

"Why did you say what you did?"

"I wanted to make sure you fully understood my position. In a way, I feel as if I'm on probation in the church. I'm not baptized. I have to be careful and prudent. That includes my behavior in everything I do."

"Especially with me." It was a statement, not a question.

Eliza looked him straight in the eye. "*Ja*. Especially with you."

He sighed. "I feel like I've done you wrong somehow."

Surprise flattened her face. "Josiah, you weren't the one who got rebellious as a teen and completely messed up! That was my fault, all my fault. You did the right thing. You stayed in the community, learned a trade, got baptized. You have all kinds of pretty women who are interested in you. You should be praising *Gott*, not second-guessing yourself."

"*Ja*, I suppose." He looked glum.

"Josiah, let me ask you a personal question. You don't have to answer it."

"Fine."

"Why are you so ambivalent toward these other women? They all seem like excellent matches for you."

"I don't know!" he burst out. "I can't find fault with any of them. But there's just no chemistry."

Eliza wrestled with her conscience, then asked the next logical question. "And am I the reason you don't feel this chemistry?" She held her breath, waiting for his answer.

"*Nein. Ja. Nein.*" He slumped against the seat back and held his head. "I don't know…"

"I'm going to take that as a *ja*." Her heart lurched, though whether from relief or dread she wasn't sure.

"*Nein*, don't." He lifted his head and looked at her. "I was courting Jodie before you came home, and it didn't work out. Then there was Maggie, then Marion. It didn't work out with them, either. But I'll admit, seeing you again didn't help. Nor does it help that *Mamm* tries too hard to steer me away from you."

"Your mother doesn't like me." Eliza kept her voice flat and emotionless.

"*Ja*, I know. I think it just springs from a natural resentment about—about how I reacted after you left."

"I can't blame your mother, really." Eliza looked down at the small head nestled against her chest. The baby was nearly asleep, soothed by the comforting rocking motion. "My past has not been exactly stellar. I have a lot of baggage."

"But as the saying goes, church is for the sick, not the healthy."

"*Ja*, maybe, but I have a lot of sin under my belt. Leaving here was an act of willful selfishness." She dropped a kiss on her baby's head. "My only task from now on is to make sure I keep from sinning any more, and raise my baby toward baptism."

"Now let me ask you a question. You don't have to answer it. Are you going to get baptized?"

Surprised at his bluntness, she leaned her head back and started rocking. "I don't know. Sometimes I don't think I'm worthy."

"That's for *Gott* to decide."

"Well… *Gott*, and the whole church community. And your mother has been vocal in her opposition to the idea."

He winced. "Well, I'm confident she'll change her mind…"

Eliza waved a hand. "Don't apologize, I understand her position. But it does lend weight to my decision to stay away from you, Josiah. I don't want to be the cause of a rift between you and your mother. I lost my mother when I was young, my father, too, and that may be why I became as rebellious as I did—because I didn't have the strong guidance of parents. Levy did the best he could, but he wasn't much more than a boy himself when our parents died. He had a heavy burden to raise me, and I did him wrong when I left."

"He's proud of you, you know."

"*Ja*, I know. And I'm glad to be back. But I

don't want to be in a position to pit you against your own family."

He looked her in the eye. "You keep saying these other women have such fine qualities. But Eliza, don't forget your own qualities. You've changed in so many ways, and all for the better."

"But my promise still stands. You know that, *ja*?"

"Ja." His gaze dropped. "I know that."

Eliza wondered why Josiah would be the one to be present during the storm damage. Was *Gott* testing her promise and determination to stay away from Josiah? Perhaps not. Perhaps *Gott* was just giving her—and Josiah—a chance to clear the air. At least he now understood her position.

Mercy had fallen asleep. "I think I'll put her down and sweep up this mess," she said. "Levy and Jane are going to be horrified enough as it is."

"Ja, *gut* idea." Josiah looked at the chaos. "The rain has stopped. I'll see about getting that branch out of here and putting something over the window opening."

For the next half hour, they were busy. Eliza swept up the glass and splintered wood from the smashed window frames. Josiah tried moving the branch, but it was too large. He seized a saw and began cutting it into pieces.

Others in the community seemed to be doing the same. In the distance, she heard hammers, and she saw the bishop and his wife riding by, their wagon filled with downed tree limbs.

In the midst of this industry, Eliza heard the rapid clip-clop of horse hooves coming closer. She saw Levy stop the buggy before the barn doors, open them and drive the horse and buggy inside. Within a few minutes, her brother and sister-in-law walked into the kitchen from the side door and gasped.

"It was that huge branch," explained Eliza.

"We didn't even know a storm had hit!" Levy's jaw dropped as he surveyed the damage. "There was a little rain in the city, but not much."

"It hit us dead-on," explained Josiah. Sawdust covered his shirt and trousers from sawing through the thick branch. "Lots of damage."

"And you're hurt," Jane said to Eliza.

"Just some cuts from flying glass. Mercy was on the other side of the room, so she didn't get hurt at all."

"Oh." Jane put her hands over her face and swayed.

"Whoa!" Levy leaped over to his wife and assisted her to a chair.

"Don't worry, Jane." Josiah looked distressed. "It looks bad, but we can get things fixed up without a problem. I even have some spare windows I can use to replace what broke."

˙ "*Danke*, Josiah." Jane's voice was shaky.

"Let's go take a look at the damage to the construction area," Levy told Josiah.

The men left the room, and Eliza sat down near Jane. "Don't let this worry you," she advised. "You have a *boppli* inside you. You need to be calm."

"*Ja*, I know." Jane groped in the pocket of her loose dress for a handkerchief. She wiped her eyes. "But it was a shock. We had no idea about the storm. How did you get hurt?"

"I was standing right next to the windows when a huge gust of wind tore the branch off," she explained. "It fell on the new roof of the house extension, then sort of rolled and bounced right into the window." She patted Jane's hands. "It looks worse than it is, though I'll probably feel bruised tomorrow. I'm just so thankful Mercy wasn't hurt."

"And that Josiah was here."

"*Ja*. He held Mercy while I got cleaned up, calmed her down." She fiddled with the edge of her apron. "We had a long talk and cleared the air."

"*Ja, gut*. I'm glad." Jane put a hand over her midsection and drew a deep breath.

"Are you okay?" Eliza watched her sister-in-law with concern.

"It's just a shock, that's all." She looked out the window where Levy and Josiah were gesturing and pointing at the damage to the house extension. "This is going to be hard on our finances, too."

"*Gott* will provide," soothed Eliza. "I'll keep making dolls since they're selling so well."

What she didn't mention to Jane was how much the storm might have damaged their crops. Her sister-in-law had enough on her plate as it was.

Chapter Eight

In the middle of the night, Eliza heard a knock on her bedroom door. Mercy stirred in her crib, but didn't wake up.

"Hmm, what?" Eliza mumbled. She rolled over, slid out of bed, and padded to the door.

Levy stood in the dark hallway, holding a kerosene lamp in one hand. "I'm taking Jane to the hospital."

Eliza snapped awake. "What's wrong?"

"She's having pain. The shock of the storm damage hit her pretty hard." He pinched the bridge of his nose. "I didn't even want to tell her how the crops fared."

"One worry at a time, Levy," she told him. "That's one thing I learned out in the *Englisch* world. Right now your priority is Jane's health, and the *boppli* she's carrying. Do you need help getting her there?"

"No, there's nothing you can do. She's getting dressed. I'm going to go hitch up the buggy. I just wanted to let you know."

He departed down the hallway, lamp in hand. Eliza bit her lip for a moment, then snatched her bathrobe off its hook and shrugged it over her nightgown. She winced as the bruises she hadn't noticed from yesterday's dramatic incidents caught up with her. Her whole body was sore, but that was nothing next to the dreaded thought of Jane losing her baby. She went downstairs to Levy's bedroom.

The door was open. Jane, fully dressed, was fastening her *kapp* over her hair. In the dim light of the kerosene lamp, her eyes looked shadowed and frightened.

"How bad is it?" asked Eliza, trying to keep her voice calm.

"Bad enough that we don't want to take any chances." Jane finished with her *kapp* and wrapped both hands over her middle in a protective gesture. "It was Levy's idea to take me to the hospital."

"Levy's right. Don't even hesitate."

"But today is Friday. It's the day we normally spend getting ready for the farmers market. If this prevents us from selling at the market tomorrow, we'll lose a lot of money, and now we have the house repairs to pay for…"

"That's what I'm here for." Eliza gave her a ghost of a smile. "I can get everything ready for the farmers market."

Jane raised her head and Eliza saw some of the worry clear from her brow. "*Ja*, you're right. I'm not thinking straight." She leaned over and kissed Eliza on the cheek. "Every day I thank *Gott* you're my sister."

Eliza's eyes prickled. "Same here."

Levy came through the kitchen toward the master bedroom. "Ready, *lieb*?"

"*Ja*, I'm ready." Jane snatched her cloak off its hook.

"I'll pray," offered Eliza as her brother escorted his wife out the door. A few moments later, the horse clip-clopped down the darkened street, with two oil lamps lit at the corners of the buggy.

The house settled into an oppressive silence. Eliza wandered through the living room where the broken windows were covered with cardboard, and upstairs to her bedroom. Mercy dozed in her crib. Eliza slipped back into bed, thinking she'd rest before tackling the day's chores, but sleep wouldn't come.

Instead she worried. Jane's unexpected pain in a previously blooming and healthy pregnancy was worrisome. "Please, *Gott*, let the baby be okay," she prayed.

After a while, Eliza got up, dressed and went downstairs, leaving Mercy in her crib. She lit a kerosene lamp and took it over to her sewing station. If she couldn't sleep, she might as well sew.

By the time dawn lit the room and the lamp was no longer needed, Eliza had gotten a lot of work done. She also had time to think about what to do for tomorrow's farmers market.

She'd never operated the booth by herself, and wondered if she could. Not with Mercy, though. She would have to ask someone to watch her baby so she could concentrate on customers. She fretted over handling everything herself. For one thing, she wasn't entirely certain she could set up the booth itself without assistance. Levy was always so competent when it came to that sort of thing.

She peeked in at Mercy, but the baby still slept. Eliza glanced out the window toward the garden plots and decided to see for herself how much damage had been wrought by yesterday's storm.

Anxious to start repairs to the storm damage, Josiah arrived early to Levy's house, just after the sun peeked over the horizon. He also wanted to see how Eliza felt after yesterday's disaster.

But no one answered his knock. In fact, the

farm seemed eerily quiet—until he noticed a solitary female figure out in the garden. He picked his way past debris from the tree branch and walked toward the vegetable plots, among flattened tomato plants and pushed-over corn. There was no question some of the vegetables were in bad shape—the corn especially—but in the early-morning light he saw many of the hardy plants already beginning to recover. There was hope.

It seemed Eliza hadn't heard his approach. *"Guder mariye,"* he said. "How bad is it?"

She whirled, a hand to her chest. Her eyes had dark circles under them. *"Guder mariye.* You're here early."

"Ja, I wanted to get a start on replacing the windows. Levy asked me to. How bad is it?" he repeated, gesturing around the garden plots.

"Bad, but it could be worse. I think we'll lose some of the corn, though. Josiah, you should know—Levy took Jane to the hospital a few hours ago."

Worry clutched his midsection. "Is it the baby?"

"Ja. The shock of coming home to a damaged house was a lot for her. She was having pains. Levy wasn't taking any chances. Jane was also fretting because today is Friday, the day they normally get everything ready for the farmers

market. I told her I'd take care of things and even do the market tomorrow if need be."

"Can you?" asked Josiah. "What about setting up the booth, that kind of thing?"

"I'll just have to make do." Eliza bit her lip.

"I'll help." He spoke without hesitation. "I'm sure I can figure out how to assemble and disassemble the booth, and together we can set it up. My mother can watch Mercy during the day."

She compressed her lips. "Will she want to? She doesn't like me…"

"But she likes Levy and Jane, and this is helping them out. During times of crisis, we all have to pitch in, *ja*?"

"Ja." Eliza turned to scan the vegetables. *"Danke*, Josiah."

After that, the day was busy beyond belief. Josiah watched Eliza with increasing respect bordering on awe. He knew she had never been solely in charge of Friday's preparation work, but she figured out what to do.

With Mercy either in her sling or toddling along in the garden, she harvested fruits and vegetables and stacked them in crates in the shady barn. She dug early potatoes and carrots. She picked late raspberries and a few early blueberries.

When she disappeared into the house, she must have started baking because the smell of fresh bread and pies soon had his mouth watering as the wonderful aromas filled the air.

Josiah supervised the work crew. He started by replacing the windows and fixing the damaged woodwork on the side of the house. Then he instructed them to clean up and do repairs to the damaged construction area, while he pitched in to help Eliza.

"Corn," she replied, when he asked what he should do first. "Pick as many ripe ears of corn as you can find. I don't know how much Levy brings every week, but I assume if it's ripe, it gets picked."

"The wind really did a number here." Josiah stared out at the tall stalks flattened by yesterday's gale.

"*Ja.* I think this more than anything caused Levy to not tell Jane the extent of the damage. But it seems the corn got the worst of it. Everything else seems okay, or will recover." She gestured toward the tomatoes.

By evening, after the rest of the work crew had gone home, Josiah stacked a crate of vegetables in the cool barn. Eliza took Mercy out of the sling and let the toddler wander in the barn amid the crates of produce.

"*Ach*, I'm tired," she admitted, and leaned backward, stretching out her back.

"Does Levy pack the wagon Friday evening

or Saturday morning?" Josiah stopped to stretch out his own back.

"Mostly Friday evening. That way he only has to load the most delicate things, such as raspberries and baked items, in the morning."

Josiah took off his hat, wiped sweat from his forehead and replaced it. "Then let's get started."

"The booth goes in last," she reminded him. "That way it's easy to unload first."

"Ja, gut."

Eliza climbed into the wagon, and he hoisted up crates of produce for her to stack. He also kept a watchful eye on Mercy as the baby wandered through the barn. Vaguely he heard the sound of hooves clip-clopping toward the house, but it wasn't until Levy called "Whoa!" that he realized Eliza's brother was home.

"Mercy!" Eliza vaulted from the wagon. "Come to *Mamm* and let Uncle Levy bring in the horse."

But Levy did not bring the buggy into the barn. Instead he unhitched the horse and led him toward the corral behind the barn for food and water.

"What news?" demanded Eliza. "How's Jane?" She swung Mercy up on her hip and followed as he led the horse. Josiah trotted after them.

"On bed rest." Levy pumped the handle and

watched the water gush into the tank. The horse put his nose in and drank. "The doctor wants to keep her through tomorrow."

"Then it's a *gut* thing you brought her in." Eliza scrubbed a hand over her face. "Thank *Gott* you brought her in," she repeated.

"*Ja*, I agree." He looked strained. "But I can't stay with her. I needed to get home and get ready for tomorrow's farmers market."

"No," said Josiah. "Go back and stay with Jane. Eliza and I have everything under control."

"You do?" Levy looked at him blankly. Josiah recognized how bone-weary the other man was.

"*Ja*. Come see."

Leaving the horse to drink, Levy followed him into the barn, where stacks of crates surrounded the wagon.

Levy stopped dead in his tracks. "I... I..." he croaked.

Josiah grinned at him. "Surprised?"

"*Ja*. Very. I had geared myself up to work all night long if necessary, picking and harvesting."

"I told Jane this morning I could handle it," offered Eliza. "But I think she was too scared and distracted to remember. Josiah fixed up the broken windows already, and the crew repaired the damage to the house expansion while he worked in the garden plots."

"*Danke*, Josiah." Levy shook his hand. Josiah thought he saw a gleam of moisture in Levy's eyes.

"Also, Levy, the storm didn't do as much damage to the garden as you think," Eliza said. "A lot of the corn got flattened, but everything else looks like it will recover."

"*Gott ist gut,*" he mumbled. He still looked dazed and relieved.

"Since you're not thinking clearly, here's what I suggest." Eliza's voice was firm. "Go back and spend the night in the hospital. I think that will be half the battle for Jane, having you there. You can assure her we've got things under control here."

"What about Mercy?" Levy touched the top of his niece's head.

"I'll ask my mother to watch her," said Josiah. "I'll tell her tonight, and we can drop the *boppli* off on the way to the market early tomorrow morning."

He saw a leap of awareness in Levy's eyes at the suggestion. "Will she agree?" he asked.

"She likes you and Jane," Josiah replied. "I'm sure she'll be happy to pitch in."

Levy looked like a fifty-pound weight had lifted off his shoulders. "*Vielen Dank*, both of you," he said. "I'm going to feed the horse and get a change of clothes, then I'll head back to the hospital."

He disappeared out the back barn door. Josiah caught Eliza's eye. *"Danke,"* she said simply. "You made my brother's burden so much lighter."

He touched his hat brim. "Glad to help."

Eliza was up at four o'clock the following morning. While Mercy slept, she fed the livestock and milked the cows. She lugged out her boxes of dolls for sale and crammed them in the wagon, along with neatly packaged breads, muffins and pies. She hadn't been able to make as many as Jane usually did, but at least there was some inventory to sell, and she'd increase the prices to bring in more money. She packed a hamper of lunch for her and Josiah. She also packed a diaper bag to leave with Ruby Lapp, with a change of clothes for Mercy, diapers, bottles of formula in an insulated pack and some of her daughter's favorite playthings.

By the time Josiah knocked at the kitchen door, Mercy was awake and Eliza was feeding her breakfast in the high chair.

"Guder mariye. Have you eaten?" she asked.

"Ja, danke. And my mother is expecting Mercy, so there won't be a problem."

She eyed him. "How did she take it?"

He shrugged. "She saw the logic of my arguments."

"I see." Eliza turned back to her daughter, her conscience searing at the thought of leaving her child with a woman who clearly didn't like her. But she knew Ruby would do her duty, however grudgingly, and Mercy would be in competent hands. "Well, I'm grateful to her. I'm almost done here, and we should be ready to go in a few minutes."

"Then I'll go hitch up the horse." Josiah departed.

Eliza tucked Mercy into her sling, then staggered outside under the added burden of the diaper bag and lunch hamper as Josiah guided the horse and loaded wagon out of the barn.

"Let me help." He jumped down from the wagon seat and relieved her of the bag and basket, piling them on top of the rest of the items in the wagon. He climbed back on the seat, took Mercy and extended a hand to assist Eliza up.

"Danke." She stepped into the wagon seat with his assistance. The courteous gesture was no more than that, Eliza reminded herself as she took Mercy onto her lap. Her hand tingled where it had touched his.

Josiah clucked to the horse.

"I'll have to do something nice for your mother in exchange for watching Mercy," she commented as the morning sun dappled through the maples on the quiet street.

"Get her some ginger."

"Excuse me?"

"She asked for some gingerroot, if there's any for sale at the farmers market."

"*Ja, gut!* I'll find her the biggest and best ginger I can!"

Josiah chuckled. "I know things haven't been easy between you, but my mother isn't all that bad. She's just had a hard time adjusting since my father passed away."

"Is she upset that you're helping me at the farmers market today?"

"Maybe," he admitted. "But she knows it's necessary. We've all had times we've had to rely on others for help. She had many people helping her when *Daed* died, and she knows this is a time to step up to the plate and help Levy and Jane."

"I'm grateful to her. And to you. I realize now I couldn't do it by myself, especially with Mercy." She hugged her baby closer.

"It's funny how busy Levy is during the summer, and yet all winter his schedule is much more relaxed."

"Their *boppli* isn't due until December, so they'll be able to get used to being parents during their slow season. It's an adjustment, having a baby."

"Especially on your own." He glanced at her.

She kept her eyes on the horse's ears ahead of her. "*Ja*, especially on my own."

Josiah's family house loomed ahead. Eliza felt unsure. "Should I just give you Mercy to take in, or bring her in myself?"

"We'll both bring her in. I'll carry the diaper bag."

They disembarked in the back of the house. Before they had a chance to knock, Ruby opened the door, waiting for them.

"Ruby, *Vielen Dank* for watching Mercy today." Eliza kept her voice firm and her chin raised.

"*Ja*, sure, what choice did you have? I know Levy is busy this time of year, and Jane needs care." The older woman held out her arms for the toddler.

"This nice lady will watch you today, *liebling*," she told her daughter. "Be *gut*, *ja*?"

Rather to her surprise, Mercy transferred over to Ruby without an issue. Josiah deposited the diaper bag inside the doorway.

"I have a little surprise for you in the kitchen," Ruby crooned to the toddler. "Would you like to see it?"

Little Mercy nodded, her eyes wide. Ruby caught Eliza's eye and jerked her head toward the wagon, gesturing they should leave while the child was distracted.

Eliza nodded and turned away. She and Josiah climbed back onto the wagon seat, and he turned the horse around and headed down the road.

Eliza blew out a breath. "I hope for your *mamm*'s sake Mercy behaves herself today. Toddlers are tricky at this age and don't always take to strangers. I'm surprised she didn't cry when we left."

"*Mamm* is *gut* with babies. Mercy will be fine."

"So now it's time to put that worry aside, and concentrate on setting up the booth and selling all day."

He glanced at her. "Are you nervous?"

"Maybe a little. Jane and Levy have told me how things are done, but I've never done it myself, and certainly never been in charge of things before. I hope I don't mess it up."

"We'll muddle through."

"Josiah… I know I've said it before, but *Vielen Dank* for doing this. I know it means a lot to Levy and Jane."

He shrugged it off. "We must all pitch in when necessary."

The farmers market was held in a shady park that took up nearly one entire city block in an otherwise quiet residential neighborhood. A section was fenced off for Amish horses and buggies, and the parking lot was for vendors only. The park was busy with farmers and merchants unloading carts, trucks, wagons and cars. Josiah pulled the horse alongside the area reserved for Levy's space, and Eliza helped unload the booth components.

"This is fastened here," she said. "And the awning is set up this way, I think."

Together, they managed to get the stall assembled without too much trouble, though it made Eliza realize she could never have done it alone.

With the clock ticking toward opening, they unloaded crates of produce and boxes of dolls and baked goods. Eliza began arranging everything. She wasn't sure where things normally went, but in the end the display looked attractive. Meanwhile, Josiah drove the wagon to the fenced field reserved for Amish vehicles and their horses, where the animal could relax for the day under the shade trees.

By the time he returned, Eliza had gotten most of the booth stocked, and had even sold some tomatoes to an early buyer.

"I think that's everything." Eliza finished arranging her dolls in their designated area. "*Ach*, what a lot of work this is. No wonder Levy and Jane are so tired every Sabbath."

"Let's hope we do them justice. Good morning," he added as a customer walked in, looking for fresh corn and happy to see early potatoes for sale.

A grandmotherly woman came in and was thrilled to spot the dolls. She purchased two sets of boy and girl dolls for her grandchildren. "Such beautiful toys," she cooed as she paid for them.

"Thank you. It's fun making them," Eliza replied, smiling.

The morning rush of customers kept them busy for a solid couple of hours. When at last they had a break, Eliza told Josiah, "I'm going to that booth over there." She pointed. "I think they sell gingerroot."

"*Ja*, sure." He smiled. Eliza knew he was aware she wanted to make a good impression on his mother.

Sure enough, the booth sold ginger. Eliza purchased five of the cleanest, fattest roots she could find and tucked them into a paper bag.

She returned to the booth in time to see Josiah selling a pair of her dolls to a woman with a small daughter in tow. Delighted, she watched the woman present the boy and girl figures to the child, who clutched them to her chest.

"That makes about half your inventory sold already," he told her.

"I must admit, there's a rush that comes with seeing them sell so well," she replied. "It's one thing to make them and have Jane and Levy sell them. It's another thing to sell them myself."

"Are you Eliza Struder?"

Surprised, Eliza turned to see a middle-aged man in neat, casual clothes. *"Ja."*

"At last, I have a chance to meet you." He held out a hand to shake. "My name is Christopher Morris."

Baffled, Eliza returned the gesture. "Do I know you?"

"No, but I've talked with your brother and sister-in-law many times. I wanted to discuss your dolls." He gestured toward the inventory.

"Ah!" Eliza's brow cleared. *"Ja,* sure, my brother mentioned you. You're the wholesale man, right?"

"That's right." He handed her a business card. "I specialize in handmade toys and represent a number of businesses in the region." He picked up a faceless figure. "These are some of the best-made Amish dolls I've ever seen. I am certain, Miss Struder, that I could make you a wealthy woman from the sale of these dolls."

A wealthy woman. Is that what she wanted? She caught Josiah's eye for a moment and saw worry.

She turned back to the man. "Let's talk, Mr. Morris."

Chapter Nine

Josiah was quiet as the day wore on, speaking mostly to customers. Eliza was baffled by the abruptness of his cold-shoulder behavior.

By closing time, she felt weary. Her legs ached from standing, her back from bending, and even her face hurt from smiling so much at potential customers. When the farmers market emptied, she went about stacking the empty crates and dismantling the displays without a word. Josiah's silence chafed at her nerves.

When the wagon was loaded with crates and the disassembled booth, she climbed into the seat and Josiah clucked to the horse.

"What's the matter?" she ventured.

"Nothing."

"You're lying, Josiah. You've barely said two words to me for the last couple of hours. What's wrong?"

"Nothing."

"Fine. Whatever." Annoyed, she turned her head and watched the passing sights.

Ten minutes went by in silence. Finally he blurted, "Is that what you want? To become a wealthy woman?"

Startled, she turned toward him. "What? Where did that come from?"

"It's what that man, Christopher Morris, said he could do for you. Is that what you want? To be wealthy?"

"Josiah, that was just sales talk. No one can become wealthy by making dolls."

"You didn't answer my question. Do you want to be wealthy?"

"No." She crossed her arms. "I want to be able to support myself and my daughter. I'm a single mother, Josiah. *Ja*, I'm living with Levy and Jane, but that doesn't mean I should fold my hands and expect my brother to support me. If there's one thing I learned in the *Englisch* world, it's that single mothers face a great deal of hardship. If I can make a living sewing dolls for that man, what do you care?"

"Money can be dangerous. It can be seductive."

"It can also make the difference between living in comfort and living in poverty," she retorted. Her temper flared. "I know that first-hand when I had Mercy. Why do you think Levy works so hard all summer long? You saw yourself how much he sells each Saturday at the farmers market. He squirrels away all the money from the summer to carry him through slower times in the winter. He has a wife and soon a child to support. Now he'll have hospital bills, too, from Jane's stay. Do you accuse him of wanting to be wealthy?"

"No…"

"Then don't presume to accuse me. You have your own construction business. You do it to earn a living. I make dolls to earn a living, and you have no right to question my goals or plans."

"But I keep my business within the Plain community. This *Englisch* man, he would bring your business outside, to the *Englisch* world."

"Who do you think I'm selling to at the farmers market?"

"It's not the same thing."

"It most certainly is. Josiah, what's gotten into you?"

"Nothing." He clamped his mouth shut and said no more.

Eliza could feel her cheeks heat up with suppressed anger. Of all the things to object to, this was the most absurd. She had tucked the wholesaler's business card in the lunch hamper.

She intended to write to him about additional details of his offer.

When Josiah pulled up in front of his house, Eliza snatched up the bag of gingerroots she had bought for his mother. She climbed down from the wagon, took a deep breath and plastered a smile on her face.

"*Ach*, she was fine," responded Ruby to Eliza's question about the baby's conduct. "We played games, she took two naps, didn't fuss at all."

"*Mamm!*" Mercy toddled up and held out her arms.

Eliza swung the baby up. "There's my *liebling*! I hear you were such a good girl for Mrs. Lapp." She turned to Ruby. "*Vielen Dank* for your help. Josiah said you might like some ginger, so I got some for you at the market." She proffered the paper bag.

"*Ach, danke.*" The older woman smiled. "I like using ginger in several dishes."

While a truce seemed in order with the mother, no such armistice existed with the son. Josiah held Mercy while she swung the diaper bag into the wagon and climbed back into the seat. She took Mercy into her lap. Josiah said nothing more as he drove back to Levy's farm.

"They're home from the hospital," she observed as he turned the horse toward the barn.

Levy emerged from the house as Josiah called "Whoa!" and pulled the animal to a stop.

"How's Jane?" asked Eliza before she even climbed down from the wagon seat.

"Fine." Levy stretched out his arms to take his niece. "Feeling much better, especially after seeing how much repair work was done on the house." He nodded to Josiah. "Words can't convey my gratitude for everything you've done."

The younger man offered a smile, the first Eliza had seen since the market. "*Ja*, sure, glad to help. I'll just head home. Eliza can fill you in on what happened today. I'll be here on Monday, bright and early."

He hopped down from the wagon, shook Levy's hand and walked away toward his own home.

Levy stared after him. "Is he okay?"

"*Ja*, just annoyed at me." She sighed and climbed down from the wagon, then took Mercy back in her arms. "I'll explain later. Let me give Mercy to Jane, and I'll help unload the wagon."

"No, don't. I can handle it. You've done enough today, Eliza. Go inside."

She nodded, hitched Mercy higher on her hip and entered the house.

Jane sat at the kitchen table, sipping tea. She smiled at her sister-in-law. "*Guten Tag!*"

Eliza put Mercy down and bestowed a hug on Jane. "How are you feeling?"

"Much better. I feel bad I caused such a fuss."

"No! It was far better you got checked out. The *boppli* inside you is okay?"

"*Ja.* The doctor did suggest I go easier on my workload, though, so I'm still trying to figure out how to do that."

"I'll pitch in on whatever I can. Perhaps we can swap some duties—you can watch Mercy while I do some of your work, that kind of thing."

"*Danke.* We'll figure something out. How did the market go?"

"It went fine. We sold well. I'll tell you all about it when Levy comes in."

"Dinner is almost ready. If you can finish preparing the food, I'll set the table."

Eliza bustled around, listening as Jane told her about the hospital stay. Levy came in a few minutes later and they sat down for the meal.

After the silent prayer, Levy reached for a bowl. "So tell me how the market went today."

Eliza blew out a breath. "Well, first of all I'm astounded by how much work you two do. I knew it in theory, of course, but it's a whole different matter to be fully in charge of sales from start to finish."

She told how Josiah and the crew had repaired

the windows and the house damage. "Then he turned the construction crew over to the house expansion and spent all day yesterday helping me pick produce and pack it in crates. Then early this morning we took off for the market. We dropped Mercy at his mother's, set up the booth and got nearly everything sold."

"No problems?" inquired Levy.

"Not really. I mean, a few glitches here and there while we figured out how to set up the booth, but that was about the worst of it. Everyone asked after you. I don't have your sales personality, that's certain sure. You have an excellent touch with customers that I lack."

"That's what I thought, too, when I first saw him in action," put in Jane. "He's a completely different person when he sells."

"Lessons from fellow vendors, that's all," replied Levy. "But if everything went so well, why was Josiah in such a sour mood a few minutes ago?"

"Sour mood?" asked Jane. "What do you mean?"

"He was out of sorts," explained Levy. "He just said he'd be here bright and early Monday morning, and left. Eliza, you said he was annoyed at you. Why?"

"I'm not sure myself." She drew her eyebrows together in a frown. "This is what happened.

The wholesale man showed up at the booth and introduced himself. He said he would be very interested in purchasing my dolls, but the term he used made Josiah uncomfortable. He said, 'I could make you a wealthy woman from the sale of these dolls.' That phrase put Josiah off."

"No one can become wealthy by hand-sewing dolls…" began Jane in bewilderment.

"*Ja*, I know. But it wasn't the dolls, it was the idea of making a lot of money that disturbed him. But I told him I'm a single mother and must support my child, and he shouldn't be judgmental if I choose to do it by sewing."

Levy looked confused. "But Josiah and I are both businessmen. We do what we must to earn money and support ourselves. We aren't wealthy, but we get by. Why does he find that offensive?"

"If I took a guess, I'd say it has more to do with my background in the *Englisch* world, where money and worldly things have more importance." Eliza sighed. "So I lost my temper and told him I make dolls to earn a living, and he has no right to question my goals or plans. After that, he gave me the silent treatment. Which, frankly, was probably a *gut* thing or I might have said worse."

Levy's eyes crinkled. "You always did have a temper, little sister."

Her brother's humor helped put things in perspective. She smiled. "*Ja*, so I did. I guess I haven't changed."

Jane chuckled. "So are you going to sell your dolls through this wholesaler?"

"I don't know." Eliza broke up a biscuit and scattered it on Mercy's high chair tray. "I've gotten faster at making them, a lot faster, but I'm running at full capacity right now, with sales at the farmers market as well as your uncle's store. I don't know if I could handle another customer."

"But remember, the farmers market ends in the fall," Levy observed. "And the sales in the Troyers' store may not last much beyond the Christmas rush. Maybe you can spend the winter and spring building up inventory."

"*Ja*, that's an idea!" Eliza's brow cleared. "I don't know why I didn't think of that."

"Because you're just starting your business, that's why." Jane took a bite of mashed potato and spoke with her mouth full. "What a pity you can't hire someone to help sew."

"Who could I hire? It's one thing to sew for a family. It's another thing to sew as a business. Most women are too busy raising their children to partner with me."

"Did this wholesaler give you a deadline of

any sort?" asked Levy. "Did he say 'I need one hundred dolls by such-and-such a date'?"

"No. And I didn't agree to anything, I just took his card and told him I'd think about it."

"Well, *Gott* will provide an answer as well as the means," said Jane. She wiped her mouth and put her napkin on the table. "*Ach*, I'm glad tomorrow is the Sabbath. There's no church service, so we can just stay home and rest."

"*Ja*, that will be wonderful." Eliza sighed. "I didn't realize a week could be so busy."

Jane rose. "Let's wash up. It's a lovely evening for sitting on the porch."

"Why don't you and Levy take Mercy out on the porch?" countered Eliza. "I'll wash up. Remember, the doctor said you need to take it easy."

"But…"

"She's right." Levy rose and lifted Mercy out of her high chair. "Let's go sit on the porch."

Outnumbered, Jane smiled her thanks at Eliza. "*Danke*. We'll keep an eye on Mercy." She departed for the porch, taking the toddler with her.

Alone, Eliza tidied the kitchen and thought about her doll business. Levy's suggestion to spend the winter months building up inventory was a good one. But could she increase the number of dolls she made now, during the busy summer months?

She doubted it. With Jane under doctor's orders not to work so hard, Eliza suspected she'd be taking over many of Jane's tasks in making jams and baked goods for the farmers market. If Jane took over watching Mercy, Eliza knew she could get a lot more done, but still…

Gott would provide an answer. Jane was right. She would put her trust in *Gott* in this matter, as she had in all other matters in her life. She wiped down the table and went to join her family on the porch.

Josiah walked back to the house he shared with his mother. Eliza's criticism stung. *Don't presume to accuse me*, she'd said. *You have no right to question my goals or plans.*

She was right, of course. So why did the notion of her making dolls for the *Englisch* wholesaler bother him so much?

Deep down, he knew it was because it was a connection to the *Englisch* world once again, a world that had pulled her away once and might pull her away again.

It's different now, he chastised himself. Before, she had been a rebellious teen. Now she was an adult and a mother. The lure wasn't the same.

But it bothered him still.

He walked up to the house. Seeing his mother through the screen door of the kitchen, he called, "I'm going to do the chores, I'll be right in."

"Ja, danke," Ruby replied.

He fed and watered the horses and chickens, poured in a bit of grain for the one remaining cow they owned. He sat down to milk the complacent animal. After his father died two years ago, his mother had a hard time keeping up with five cows, so they reduced their herd to just a cow and a calf.

His father. Watching the warm sweet milk zing into the pail, he thought with fondness of the man who'd raised him and taught him everything he knew about the carpentry profession. The legacy allowed him to start his own business to support himself and his mother. Now the older man was gone, and Josiah missed him fiercely. How much worse was it for his mother, who had lost her husband of thirty years?

And Eliza. She had no such legacy of parental support. She'd lost her parents at such a young enough age that many of the skills that would have passed from mother to daughter had to be acquired mishmash from others in the church community. Levy had done his best to raise his younger sister, but he couldn't teach her to sew. No wonder she took such pleasure in her burgeoning doll business. The skills she cultivated were hard-won.

He finished the milking, slapped the cow affectionately on her flank and released her to the pasture for the evening.

Ruby had dinner on the table for him. "How went the farmers market?" she inquired after the silent blessing.

"Fine. Busy. I don't think I ever realized how much work Levy and Jane put into that booth. Nearly every customer inquired after them and expressed concern for Jane."

"And Jane—is she okay?"

"*Ja.* Levy said she's fine. I suspect she'll have to go easier, though. I'm sure she and Eliza are figuring out a different work schedule right now. Doubtless Eliza will have to pick up a lot of the slack."

"Doubtless." Ruby concentrated on her food.

"How did you get on watching the baby?" asked Josiah. "It's the first in a long time you've had to watch a young one."

"She was a *gut* baby, no trouble at all," admitted Ruby. "We played the same kind of kitchen games I played with your sisters when they were the same age. She napped twice and didn't cry." The older woman paused. "Eliza seems to be doing a *gut* job raising her, despite everything."

"*Ja*, I agree. And she's a sweet baby." He felt a glow of affection for the toddler.

"I guess…"

"*Mamm.*" Josiah laid down his fork. "Eliza is working hard to raise her child, to support her and earn her keep with Levy and Jane. She even has interest in her dolls from an *Englischer* who could make her more money. She's industrious and kind. Why do you dislike her so much?"

"I don't dislike her…"

He waved her quiet. "*Ja*, you do. I realize she had a wild stretch when she left and went into the *Englisch* world, but she learned her lesson and returned. She's behaved herself since she came home. Yet you've never let go of your hostility toward her."

"I'm not hostile…" began Ruby.

"*Ja*, you are. But why?"

His mother looked stubborn. "Because… Because… I have my doubts she'll stay."

"What has she said or done to make you think that?"

She was silent, her brows furrowed. Instead of answering, she countered, "Why are you so interested in her?"

"You know we liked each other when we were younger. The pull is still there," he admitted.

"You can't court a woman like that!"

"A woman like what?" Josiah clamped down on his temper.

"A woman with a past. A woman who left the Amish. A woman with a baby."

"A woman who overcame a great deal, grew up in a hurry, was married and widowed, and returned to her roots," he snapped. "A woman who still has to face down a great deal of community disapproval and fight for the *gut* reputation she now carries."

"She's a wild woman, Josiah! You can't possibly be interested in someone like that."

"That must be my decision, *Mamm*. Not yours. Is there no room in you for forgiveness? Our faith is strong, and it includes forgiveness and redemption."

"But are you sure her redemption is complete?"

"As far as I can see, *ja*. But again, why are you so hostile toward Eliza? She's never done anything wrong to you, has she?"

"No… No. But just compare her to someone like Jodie. Or Maggie. Or Marion. Now *those* are women who would make any man a *gut* wife. Calm, sweet, peaceful…"

"Boring." Josiah blurted the word, then made a motion as if to snatch it back.

Ruby looked almost panicked. "You can't court Eliza!"

"I didn't say I was going to court her. But neither can I deny the spark between us. Would you have me marry someone I don't love with all my heart? Marriage is forever. Jodie and Maggie and Marion are *gut* women and there is much I admire about them. But they're not right for me."

"Don't say that!"

"Why not? It's the truth." Baffled, Josiah stared at his mother's distressed face. "What's wrong?"

"You can't marry Eliza!"

"What?" Josiah wondered if his mother was all right in the head. She had the hunted look of a trapped animal. "These are things I have to decide for myself. Marriage is a lifelong commitment, and I won't be railroaded into marrying someone I don't love."

"Josiah, don't do this to me…"

"Do *what* to you?" His exasperation showed. "Why are you pressuring me away from Eliza? What's wrong?"

"Nothing." Ruby's answer was quick. Too quick. "It's just that…that she's not a *gut* match for you, and…"

"Would you push on me a woman I don't love? Would you have me marry someone that would make me unhappy? You and *Daed* knew what happiness was."

Pain sliced across his mother's face. "Don't speak to me about your father. You can't understand how difficult it was to lose him."

"I'm sorry, *Mamm*." Josiah felt his temper recede. "I know you had a very hard time adjusting to losing *Daed*."

He saw his mother's eyes fill with tears. *"Ja."* She looked at her plate. "Harder than you'll ever know." She fished a handkerchief from her pocket and mopped her face.

Josiah felt chastened. He didn't want to be on bad terms with his widowed mother. "Tell you what, you go rest. I'll wash up," he offered.

"Danke." Ruby slid out of her chair and went into the living room.

"Do you want some tea?" he called after her.

"Ja, please."

He set the kettle to heating, cleared away the food and dishes and put the kitchen to rights. Meanwhile the bizarre conversation replayed over and over in his mind. *You can't marry Eliza! Josiah, don't do this to me... She's not a gut match for you...*

Why did the exchange clang with a discordant tone in his mind? Something seemed bizarre and unreal in his mother's insistence that he leave Eliza alone, something mysterious. *Don't do this to me...*

Why would the thought of him courting Eliza

disturb his mother so much? Her resistance seemed fueled by something deeper that she wouldn't reveal. What would she do if he pursued Eliza against his mother's wishes?

There was a piece missing from the equation. He didn't like mysteries, but it seemed he was in the middle of one.

Chapter Ten

"Ah, the Sabbath," sighed Eliza with contentment. "*Gott* knew what He was doing when He ordained a day of rest."

"*Ja.*" Jane sipped a cup of tea from her rocking chair on the porch. "It helps put the whole week into perspective."

"I was thinking last night about how best to tackle this upcoming week's work," continued Eliza, setting her own chair to rocking. "You said you have a schedule you follow as far as things to make for selling at the farmers market?"

"*Ja*, sure. I try to make canned goods such as raspberry jam earlier in the week. Later in the week I make baked goods so they'll be fresher."

"What is the hardest thing for you? Physically, I mean?"

"Hmm. Probably the jams."

"I think what you might want to do is draw up a list for me. Divvy out what you think you can handle while still taking it easy, as the doctor ordered. I'll take the rest." She rubbed her chin, considering. "I still want to try to keep up with making dolls, but I may have to let go the inventory I send to your aunt and uncle's store until the summer rush is over."

"I'm sure they'll understand. Summer is busy for all of us." She smiled at her niece as Mercy carefully climbed the porch steps. "I'll just make it more of my job to watch Mercy. That won't be a hardship, will it, *liebling*?" She reached down and pulled the toddler into her thickening lap.

Eliza chuckled. "It's like she has two mothers."

"She does. I couldn't love this little one any more than if she were mine."

"And soon you'll have your own."

Jane's eyes took on a glow of love, and she glanced over at Levy, reading a book in a hammock strung between two trees. "*Ja.* One of my own. Of *our* own."

The palpable love on her sister-in-law's face made Eliza's eyes prickle. She knew she had never felt that way with Bill, her *Englischer* husband, even at her most infatuated. Her love had been stripped away fast enough when she became pregnant with Mercy and he refused to accept the serious responsibilities of impending fatherhood.

Would she ever be able to duplicate the love between her brother and his wife? Would she ever have a man to love in the same way?

She shoved aside treacherous thoughts of Josiah. She had promised *Gott* to leave him alone, and she would stick to her side of the bargain. No matter what.

"Wow. You're up early." Levy came stumbling into the kitchen early Monday morning, yawning. Eliza was engaged in sterilizing canning jars.

"*Ja.* I'm taking over a lot of Jane's chores this week, so I wanted to get an early start." She waved a hand toward a bucket of raspberries. "Besides, it was no hardship picking berries before the sun rose. It was cooler, for one thing, and for another the wasps weren't out yet."

"I'll pick more for you this morning," said Levy. "When the berries are in full bore like this, we can't let the picking go."

"And I can pick, too." Jane emerged from the bedroom off the kitchen, adjusting her *kapp*. "Picking is not hard, and the doctor won't mind."

"Does that count as 'taking it easy'?" teased Eliza.

"At least I'm not on bed rest. He just said I should get off my feet more."

"There are so many raspberries right now that I can even bring you out a chair," offered Levy. "That way you can concentrate on the lower berries, and I'll pick higher."

"*Ja, gut,* that will work. And Mercy can be outside with me. She can pick berries, too," said Jane.

"And I'll turn everything you bring in into jam," said Eliza.

"Where *is* Mercy?" asked Jane. "Is she still asleep?"

"*Ja.*" Eliza cocked her head toward the stairs, listening. "Make that no. I'll be right back."

Mercy stood in her crib, wailing with her usual early-morning crankiness. "Now, now, *liebling,*" crooned Eliza. She lifted her daughter up, laid her on the changing table and put on a fresh diaper. "Your uncle Levy and aunt Jane are already up. Do you want a bit of breakfast?"

Too sleepy to answer, Mercy buried her head in her mother's shoulder as Eliza carried her downstairs.

Levy had disappeared into the barn and Jane started breakfast. By the time Levy came in with foaming pails of milk, the table was set and the food was ready.

"Mornings like this never get old." Eliza gave Mercy a warm biscuit to gnaw. "A happy, cordial family life. I've seen the contrast, and it makes me never fail to appreciate the blessings we have."

"Gott ist gut," agreed Levy, smiling at his wife. "And having a *boppli* in the house is even better." He gently chucked Mercy under her chin.

The sound of voices came through the open window. "The crew is here early," observed Jane.

"It's getting warmer. I'm sure they're trying to beat the heat." Levy buttered a biscuit and bit into it.

Eliza fought down the familiar feeling of butterflies at knowing Josiah was near. She kept her voice level. "Jam today, and my goal this week is to make fifty dolls. I've got my daily routine, and as long as I cut out the doll parts on Monday, I'll manage."

Jane pulled a frown. "I feel guilty, pushing the heavier kitchen work on you."

"Don't feel guilty. Watching Mercy will make up for it."

"We all have our jobs to do." Levy wiped his mouth and rose. "Starting now. I'd best get to it."

The day's work set the schedule for the rest of the week. Eliza labored to make jam and snatch moments for sewing. She figured out another trick to speed up the process of making the dolls. She juggled child care duties with Jane. On Tuesday, she made chutney and worked on her sewing. On Wednesday, more jam, and she blasted through four dozen sets of doll clothes.

And each day, Eliza was conscious of Josiah working just a few yards away. Once or twice she caught his eye and nodded, but that was it. She spoke no words to him.

But she watched him. Watched his shirt darken with sweat as he tackled the building project. Watched as he directed his crew with courtesy and firmness, but with enough banter to keep the men laughing and joking as they hammered and sawed. He was a good boss, a good carpenter.

Midweek near lunchtime, she saw Jodie walk toward the house, carrying a picnic basket. Eliza paused in her work and watched the byplay. Josiah stopped hammering, and she heard him say, "You brought lunch? But I thought…"

"I know you like meat pasties. I was making some for dinner tonight and thought you might like them for lunch."

Eliza almost laughed at the expression on his face—a mixture of exasperation and guilt. "Uh, *ja, danke*." He spoke to his crew, evidently telling them to break for the midday meal. Then he removed his tool belt and went to sit with Jodie.

Eliza swallowed the hot flush of jealousy that gripped her, and turned away from the window. Would it always be this way? Jodie was persistent, Eliza gave her that, but it could have been any woman sitting there under the tree with the man she loved.

"What's wrong?"

Eliza jerked her head up. Jane stood in the kitchen doorway, watching her with concern.

"N-nothing… Where's Mercy?"

"Napping." Her sister-in-law raised an eyebrow. "You have a look of anguish on your face, and you tell me it's nothing?"

Eliza closed her eyes and jerked her head toward the window. Jane walked over, took one look at the couple sitting in the shade of the maple tree and retreated.

She laid a sympathetic hand on Eliza's arm. "No one knows more than me how awful jealousy can be," she said. "Did I ever tell you why I left my hometown and came here to Grand Creek?"

"You might have. I forget."

"Jealousy, that's what it was. The man I loved married my best friend. I couldn't bear to see their happiness, so I asked Aunt Catherine and

Uncle Peter if I could come and stay with them. They said I could work in their store, but *Gott* had other plans."

"You met Levy."

"*Ja.* To be precise, he rescued me from the train station after someone snatched my money and I was stranded. He happened to be there picking up his new booth and trying to take care of Mercy. This was just after you sent her to him, and he was beside himself since he was all thumbs with the *boppli*. He asked me if I could be Mercy's nanny until he figured out what to do." Jane smiled, and her plain face transformed into beauty. "*Gott* knew what He was doing when He sent me away from my hometown."

"Are you suggesting it would be best if I leave Grand Creek?"

A look of distress crossed Jane's face. "No! What I'm saying is to give your troubles to *Gott*. He's the only One who is able to sort things out."

Eliza slumped. "*Ja.* It's when I try to force *Gott*'s hand that things get complicated. I turned my back on *Gott* when I left the church community. I thought I could do things better on my own. I soon learned differently."

"And do you think you would be better off leaving?"

Pain clutched her heart. "No, but it's hard watching the man I love courting someone else."

"But he's *not* courting her. He's not courting anyone."

"It doesn't matter if he does or doesn't. I made a promise to *Gott* not to interfere, and I won't. Whoever he sees, that's his business. My business is to behave like an adult member of this community, and as a mother."

"But that's not easy, is it?"

"No." Eliza plucked at her *kapp* strings. "Sometimes I look at the business card of that wholesaler I met at the farmers market and wonder if I should just contact him and set up a business arrangement with him. I wonder if I could go somewhere to raise Mercy by myself, away from all the heartache."

"Not that I think you should, but what stops you?"

"Mercy." Eliza spoke promptly. "She needs to be raised with her own people, not strangers. I want to teach her not to be rebellious, as I was. If I left the town and went elsewhere, even to another Amish community as you did, it would just be running away. It would be a form of rebellion. It's up to me to chastise my own wayward heart and be mature."

"But it's a battle, *ja*?"

"Ja." Eliza closed her eyes and pinched the bridge of her nose. "It's a battle."

"Trust in *Gott*." Jane gave her a sympathetic pat on the arm. "It's what my aunt told me when I was tearing my heart out over Levy. I fought and railed against her advice, but in the end she was right."

Trust in Gott. Not easy advice, but Eliza knew she had no choice.

On Friday around lunchtime, Jane kept Mercy out of the kitchen while Eliza baked batch after batch of bread, rolls, pies and cookies. As each item cooled, she wrapped it and tucked it into boxes for the next day's farmers market. Through the kitchen window, she saw Jane playing with Mercy in the shade near the garden.

Eliza had been up before dawn, finishing a production run of dolls by lamplight, and she was tired. Sweat dripped down her face in the stifling kitchen, even though all the windows were open. She wiped her forehead with a corner of her apron.

"You're working too hard."

She turned. Josiah stood in the kitchen doorway, hammer in one hand. "Excuse me?"

"I've been watching you all week, doing double duty. You're simply working too hard."

"What choice do I have?" she snapped. *He'd been watching her...*

He shrugged. "Are you working the market tomorrow?"

"Probably. That way Jane can stay home with Mercy. It will be less tiring for her than being on her feet all day selling things."

"And you've been making dolls, too?"

"*Ja*, sure, of course."

He shook his head, but he had a smile of admiration on his face. "Amazing. I don't know how you do it."

"Time management." She pushed a stray strand of hair out of her eyes and tried not to acknowledge his flattery.

"I still think you're working too hard and should take it easy a bit more."

"I can't. There's work to be done, and we're on a strict schedule during the summer months. You know that, Josiah."

"*Ja*, I suppose I do." He leaned against the door frame, eyeing her.

Eliza became nervous. What would account for his sudden chattiness? She resumed her work, conscious of his presence.

In her forthright way, she tackled her concerns head-on. "Why the interest in what I do? I thought you were ready to throw me to the wolves after last week's market."

"*Ja*. Um, I'm sorry about that." He looked chastened. "I overreacted."

"Yes, you did. My sewing business is none of your concern. But what upset you in the first place? The wholesaler? He seems like a decent man."

"He's *Englisch*," blurted Josiah.

"*Ja*. So?"

"So, I gave in to some bad thoughts. I was afraid his business offer would lure you away again, out into the *Englisch* world."

So it was as she suspected. She shook her head. "Things are different now. I'm older. I'm a mother. I have a brother and sister-in-law who love and support me. I'm no longer a rebellious *youngie*, Josiah, and it's time everyone in this community understands and accepts that."

He opened his mouth to reply, but was interrupted.

Jodie stood in the opposite doorway, a picnic basket in hand. "What's going on?" Her eyes darted between Josiah and Eliza, a wounded expression on her face. It was clear she felt like an intruder.

To Eliza's amusement, Josiah blushed scarlet. "*Ach. Guder nammidaag*, Jodie."

The young woman's eyes filled with tears. "What's going on?" she repeated.

"Nothing. We're just talking." He bared

his teeth in a tense smile. "Did you bring me lunch?"

"Ja." She knuckled away a tear. "Unless you'd rather have lunch with *her.*" She jerked her head toward Eliza.

"Of course not," he replied.

Eliza spoke up. "This is my home, Jodie. Josiah simply had a question for me as I worked. How can you find that objectionable?"

Jodie leveled Eliza with a malevolent glare. "Because you already have a reputation."

"As what?" Eliza crossed her arms and kept her voice level. "Please, tell me."

"Never mind." Jodie's tears dried up like magic and her wounded look was replaced by a sullen expression.

An uncharitable anger burned in Eliza's chest. So she had a reputation, did she? Jodie's hostility shook her more than she wanted to admit. She had done nothing—nothing!—since returning to the church community to sully her reputation. A five-minute conversation in her own kitchen with a man her brother had hired to do some construction work wasn't enough to discredit her.

"Come." Josiah spun Jodie around and pushed her out of the kitchen.

She watched as the couple went to their usual tree and spread out the picnic lunch in its shade.

They seemed to be bickering, but she couldn't be certain.

What *was* certain was the expression on Josiah's face. He ate the food Jodie had brought, but it seemed he hardly tasted it. He looked defensive, possibly even angry. Whatever he said to Jodie didn't seem to soothe her. Instead, she seemed angry, sulky, upset.

Far sooner than normal, Jodie packed up the picnic hamper and flounced away. Josiah went back to work.

Eliza mixed another batch of cookies, thinking over the matter. Obviously Jodie was trying to press for a relationship, and just as obviously Josiah wasn't interested. A tiny bit of her was glad for his disinterest in the pretty young woman, but it didn't make her position any easier.

For some reason, her thoughts went back to the kindly pastor and his wife who had paid for her trip home after her disastrous excursion into the *Englisch* world. She had wanted to repay them for the ticket price, but they wouldn't hear of it. Instead, they asked her to "pay it forward" and do a kindness for someone else in need. She promised them she would.

But in the time since returning home, the opportunity hadn't arisen. Would it ever? It was a debt she felt keenly, a weight on her shoulders to add to other weights already pressing her down.

She didn't view her helping Jane and Levy as paying it forward. If anything, that was merely compensating them for their support. She wanted to do something unconnected to a debt she owed others.

Her hands stalled over her baking project. Was relocating the answer? That would leave Josiah free to court someone else. Jane had fled her hometown to avoid the sight of the man she loved married to her best friend. Could she do the same? There were endless Amish communities around the country, and she could find a connection with any of them. It would give her an excuse to start over, begin fresh, without the unspoken baggage of her past choices weighing her down. Her sewing business would provide the means to support them.

But the thought of Mercy held her back. Mercy was deeply loved here by people who had a vested interest in her welfare. The child was in the transition between baby and toddler and could adapt to any situation, of course, but the love that Levy and Jane lavished on the child would be impossible to replace.

Besides, running away was not the answer. She'd tried that once and regretted it.

She turned her back on the maple tree in the

yard under which Jodie had spread her picnic lunch before flouncing away. The young woman had shown a remarkable degree of immaturity, in Eliza's opinion. Yet was she, Eliza, acting with any more maturity?

Leave the community? Only a *youngie* would do something like that. And Eliza was no *youngie*. Not anymore.

Josiah banged at the nails with greater force than necessary to drive them through the wood. His crew, bless them, had witnessed the picnic argument and didn't inquire into his excessive concentration.

It was humiliating, that's what it was. He and Eliza were having a perfectly innocent conversation, and Jodie had blown it all out of proportion. He thought he'd made his position clear to her days ago—that he wasn't interested in courtship—but she was a persistent little thing. He thinned his mouth and banged another nail. He just wanted Jodie to leave him alone. He wanted all the women his mother pushed on him to leave him alone. Was that too much to ask?

Women! He nursed a momentary resentment of their feminine wiles and emotional complexity. His life used to be simple. What happened?

He paused in his work, fished out a bandanna and wiped his forehead. "Okay, I think we can start the sheathing," he told his crew. "Let's see about getting the insulation placed, too."

He worked, methodically and competently, to make progress on the project. Whatever his inner turmoil, it had nothing to do with the job at hand.

But from atop a ladder, it was easy to see into the kitchen window a few yards away, at Eliza toiling with the oven, making a variety of baked goods to sell on the morrow—all so Jane could rest and not endanger her unborn baby.

He winced and returned his attention to the task at hand. He was looking forward to the day this project was done, and he didn't have to see Eliza on a daily basis.

She was working so hard to be a *gut* woman. His daily presence was just complicating her life and his.

Chapter Eleven

"Are you sure you're up for attending the Sabbath service?" Eliza asked Jane.

"*Ja*, of course." Jane finished packing the baskets of food for the afternoon meal. "I'm feeling much better, especially since I was off my feet most of yesterday. *Vielen Dank* for working the farmers market again with Levy. That's two weeks in a row you've worked it."

"It was easy, especially since you had Mercy." Eliza hitched her daughter higher on her hip. "But *ja*, if you feel fine to go to the Sabbath services, I think Levy has the buggy hitched up."

Levy helped Jane into the buggy, then held Mercy as Eliza climbed aboard. He touched the reins to the horse's back, and the animal trotted toward the farm where the Sabbath service was being held.

"It will be *gut* to see everyone," remarked

Jane. One hand rested lightly on her thickening midsection as she watched the scenery pass.

"Ja." Eliza's voice held some doubt. "Though sometimes I imagine people still look at me cross-eyed while I'm at church."

"You know," advised Levy, "there comes a point where you have to accept that people's thoughts are their own. You've done nothing wrong since returning to the church community. If people want to think ill of you because of your past, that's their problem, not yours."

"Ja, I know. It's just advice that's easier said than done."

She let the subject drop and instead just enjoyed the beautiful morning. Levy guided the horse through the quiet roads arched over with maples and oaks. Birds sang and a soft breeze played on her face. She thought for a moment what her life was like right before Mercy was born—holed up, widowed and desperate, in a dingy apartment in the middle of a huge city. She never heard birdsong, never saw flowers waving in the breeze, never smelled fields of newly plowed earth or saw the rustle of corn as it swayed in the breeze. And now she was back where she belonged, with the people she understood. She knew she would never leave her church community again, regardless of doubts or doubters in her life.

It was in this settled frame of mind that she got down from the buggy, brought the baskets of food to the trestle tables for the meal later on and went to the women's side of the worship service. With Mercy on her lap, she seated herself between Jane and another woman with teen children.

Abruptly the older woman next to her got up without a word and reseated herself elsewhere. Surprised but not concerned, Eliza chatted in low tones to Jane until Matthew Kemp, the bishop, stood up to announce the first hymn of the service.

She focused her mind on godly matters as the service went through the beautiful old hymns and a sermon on the subject of redemption. As often happened, she felt the content was directed straight to her, and she thanked *Gott* for her own redemption. Mercy was quiet and content in her lap, and the baby was proof enough she had made the right decision to come home.

After the closing hymn, she stood up and stretched her legs. Mercy needed a diaper change, so she murmured an explanation to Jane and made her way to a quiet corner to attend to the toddler's needs.

On the way, she noticed a cluster of older women, Ruby among them, whispering with drawn faces and cutting expressions. Their voices died as she passed and revived behind her back.

A cluster of gossiping women, especially at a church service, was so unusual that a discordant note jangled Eliza's peace of mind. She laid Mercy on a small quilt and changed the child's diaper. "Are you hungry, *liebling*?" she asked, and the toddler nodded and said, *"Ja!"*

"Let's go find you some *gut* things to eat." She repacked the diaper bag, slipped Mercy into her sling and settled the child on her hip.

The family hosting the church service had set up trestle tables loaded with food in the shade of some large maple trees, and people everywhere lined up to fill their plates, chatting in subdued tones as befit the Sabbath. But as she walked, groups of women parted before her and rejoined after she passed, as if avoiding her.

She passed Ruby, who paused and muttered something in an undertone about baptism.

Startled, Eliza stopped next to the older woman. "Excuse me, what did you say?"

"You heard me." Ruby's face was pinched. "I wonder if baptism is too good for you."

"Would you care to explain what you mean by that?" Eliza kept her voice cool and polite.

"Nein. Never mind." Ruby turned her back and stalked away.

Baffled and hurt, Eliza stared after Josiah's

mother, wondering what on earth that cryptic remark meant.

She made her way toward the back of the line, and noticed the same thing—groups of chatting women fell silent as she passed and resumed their subdued gossip as she moved on. Eliza felt her face flush, though for what reason she didn't know.

She filled a plate and went to join her brother and sister-in-law, but her appetite had fled. Instead she focused on making sure Mercy had enough to eat. She longed to be home, away from the whispering women and veiled looks in her direction. What was going on? Why was there suddenly an undercurrent of hostility directed at her? What had she done?

The interminable meal ended and Eliza slipped Mercy in her sling and helped clean up the remains of the food while the men gathered up benches and loaded them in the special wagons reserved for transporting seats between Sabbath services.

Josiah passed nearby and she stopped him. "What's going on?" she asked in a low voice. "Why are people avoiding me? I'm picking up a lot of unfriendliness and I don't understand it."

"*Ja.* Me, too." He pulled off his straw hat and scratched his head in bafflement. "I'm not getting too much from the men, but I see a lot of women in clusters, whispering. It's strange."

Eliza intercepted a hostile look from Ruby. "I should get back to work," she told him, and moved away. She didn't want to cause further issues between Josiah and his mother.

But she remained confused. Last week when Ruby had watched Mercy for the day, when she and Josiah worked the farmers market, it seemed she had parted on good terms with the older woman. What could have happened to reverse the situation? She was clueless.

Hugging Mercy close, Eliza turned away and wiped a furtive tear.

She walked over to where Levy finished hitching the horse to the buggy. He helped his wife up, then held Mercy while Eliza climbed aboard. Levy seated himself, picked up the reins and clucked to the horse.

She stayed silent as Levy and Jane chatted about the service, talked about friends and discussed where the next service would be held.

It wasn't until they arrived home and Levy disappeared into the barn to unhitch and wipe down the horse that Jane turned to Eliza.

"You're awfully quiet," she remarked. "What's wrong?"

Eliza once again blessed her sister-in-law's perception. "Let's go inside," she said. "I need to talk. After I put this *liebling* down for a nap, that is."

"I'll make tea. You take care of Mercy."

Mercy lay down in her crib without protest, and Eliza lingered and sang a soft lullaby until the tired toddler closed her eyes. When she re-entered the kitchen a few minutes later, Jane had seated herself at the kitchen table with two steaming mugs before her.

"Now, what's wrong?" asked Jane.

Eliza dropped into the chair opposite. "I don't know, that's the weird thing. But all through the Sabbath service and the meal afterward, I kept intercepting odd looks and passing whispering groups of women. Maybe I'm just being para-noid, but it seemed all the women were acting very hostile. And Ruby… Well, Ruby said the oddest thing to me."

"What?"

"She said, 'I wonder if baptism is too good for you.'"

Jane startled. "What did *that* mean?"

"I don't know, and she wouldn't explain. It was…" Eliza felt her eyes well up. "It was a very uncomfortable Sabbath service, and I still don't know why people were acting so strange."

Jane shook her head. "I was so caught up in myself, I didn't even notice. I just started talking with other young mothers, gathering information about pregnancy and babies and new motherhood, that I didn't pick up any undercurrents."

"You have an advantage," observed Eliza with a shaky smile. "You don't have a past like I do. You never had any baggage you had to overcome. Even though I grew up here, I have a lot of amends to make."

Jane patted Eliza's hand. "You're right. You have amends to make."

Surprised at Jane's bluntness, Eliza turned to her. "To someone in particular?" Concern clutched Eliza's chest.

"To yourself."

"Wh-what do you mean?"

"I mean, you've been home almost a year now, but you're still walking on tenterhooks about your past, your reputation, the mistakes you made. Everyone else has forgiven you. Now you need to forgive yourself."

Was this true? Had she not forgiven herself? Eliza stared at her mug of tea, thinking about the blunders she'd made in the past. Maybe Jane was right. For how long would she beat herself up for things that were past and done, rather than looking into the future with hope and optimism?

"I never thought about it," she said slowly.

"Now, granted, if there was a cloud of hostility toward you at the Sabbath service, this doesn't explain why," Jane admitted. "But whatever people are thinking, it doesn't change the fact that you have no reason to be ashamed or embarrassed. After all, you've done nothing wrong. Just remember that. You've done nothing wrong."

"You make it seem so easy." Eliza sighed and wrapped her hands around the warm mug.

"It's *not* easy," replied Jane with a rueful smile. "The hardest part is convincing one's self about something that might not be true. I beat myself up left, right and center last summer when I was convinced Levy had no interest in me." As always, a soft look came into Jane's eyes when mentioning her husband. "*Gott* had plans for me. He has plans for you, too, Eliza. It's hard advice to take, but be patient."

Mercy took a long nap, and Eliza settled on the porch, taking advantage of the Lord's day of rest. She tried to read a book, but her thoughts wouldn't focus.

Instead, she dwelled on the subdued hostility at the Sabbath service. Puzzled over it. Worried over it. Fretted over it. Wondered where it came from. Wondered why it seemed directed at her.

She reviewed her behavior over the past two weeks and tried to pinpoint anything she might have done wrong, but could think of nothing.

The unease lingered. She didn't realize how

much she took the good opinion of others in the church community for granted until it was absent.

Down the length of the long graveled driveway, Eliza watched people stroll. Sundays were a prime opportunity to visit and chat. She saw children playing. She saw courting couples, walking together. She wondered if, somewhere, Josiah was now strolling with someone. She closed her eyes and shook her head to dispel the mental image.

She saw a solitary man walk along the road. It was the bishop, Matthew Kemp. Idly she wondered where he was going on a Sunday afternoon. Therefore it was a huge shock when he strode up the driveway, straight toward the porch.

Eliza's unease grew. She rose to her feet and laid the book aside. "*Guder nammidaag*, Bishop Kemp," she said politely. "Can I offer you a glass of lemonade?"

"*Guder nammidaag.*" He paused in the shade of a generous maple. "No thank you, I'm not here for a social visit."

"May I get Levy for you? Do you have some business to conduct with him?"

"No. I'm here to see you."

"Me?" Startled, she stared at him.

Jane and Levy emerged from the house and

stood behind her on the porch. The bishop nodded to them, but spoke to Eliza. "I wonder if I might speak to you tomorrow afternoon."

Fear clutched her, but she kept her voice steady. She nodded. "*Ja*, sure. At your office?"

"*Ja.* Two o'clock, if it's convenient for you."

Her heart battered her ribs. "I'll be there."

"*Gut.*" He touched his hat brim, turned on his heel and strode away.

Eliza stared after him, biting her lip and fighting tears.

"What was *that* about?" Levy inquired.

"I don't know." Boneless, she slid down and sat on the porch steps. "I have no idea."

Jane sat down next to her and put a sympathetic arm around her shoulders. "Do you want me to go with you tomorrow when you talk with him?"

"I don't think he wants anyone else there. He would have requested it otherwise." Eliza fished in her pocket for a handkerchief and sniffed into it. "I'm sure this has to do with everyone's attitude this morning at the Sabbath service, but I don't know what's going on or why everyone gave me the cold shoulder."

Levy leaned against a pillar. "I can't even claim it's all in your imagination," he admitted. "This sounds serious."

"What did I do?" Eliza burst out. She pounded

the porch step. "I've spent my entire time here walking the straight and narrow, and now I'm getting cryptic remarks about whether baptism is too good for me, and now the bishop wants to talk to me." A thought hit her, one so terrifying that she felt the blood drain from her face. *"Meidung,"* she moaned. "Shunning…"

Beside her, Jane froze. "No!" she cried. "He couldn't! You've done nothing to violate the rules of the *Ordnung*! He couldn't shun you!"

"What else could it be?" Eliza burst out crying, sobbing into the handkerchief. "What else could explain the gossip and whispering at the service this morning, and now the bishop wants to talk to me?"

"Eliza, calm down." Levy sat down on the porch steps on her other side. He gave her shoulders a brotherly shake. "You can't be shunned because you're not baptized. You don't know what Bishop Kemp wants to say, and you're assuming the worst."

"Ja," added Jane. "This is one instance where not being baptized may work in your favor. There's no way the bishop can implement the *meidung.*"

"Jane's right," said Levy. "And you can't go into this meeting tomorrow assuming the worst. Even if you're not yet baptized, can you honestly say you've been behaving in a way that goes against the *Ordnung*?"

Eliza hiccupped and raised her face out of the handkerchief. "No. At least, I don't think so. But then why else would he want to talk to me?"

"You won't know until tomorrow." Jane gave her a little bracing shake across the shoulders. "Come inside, I'll make you some more tea."

"Tea is a universal solution," joked Eliza weakly. She rose to her feet, and Levy propped her up when she swayed. She headed for the kitchen and dropped onto a kitchen chair.

In a few moments, Jane placed a steaming mug in front of her. "It's chamomile," she clarified. "You need something to calm you down."

Eliza nodded her thanks and wrapped her hands around the mug. Her thoughts ran around, flip-flopping from one dire scenario to the next, like a rabbit in a snare. She stared unseeing at the table.

"Liebling—" Levy sat down next to her "—you're still assuming the worst, I can tell. I'll walk with you to the bishop's tomorrow. I won't sit in on the meeting, of course, but you won't have to walk alone."

To walk alone. Eliza raised teary eyes and saw her beloved brother and sister-in-law watching her, concern written on their faces. She smiled and her mouth trembled. "Whatever happens," she said, "I thank *Gott* for both of you. I don't know what I'd do without you."

"You won't have to." Jane touched her hand for a moment. "We're here for you. And don't worry about Mercy. She'll stay here with me while you talk to the bishop."

Mercy. Eliza's dire predictions about her own fate suddenly grew worse as she considered the potential impact on her innocent daughter. She could, after all, be asked to leave the community.

But Levy was right. No sense borrowing trouble, especially since a *meidung* couldn't happen to an unbaptized person. She drew a deep, cleansing breath.

"I will pray," she said in a low voice. "Pray for calmness, pray for clarity, pray for insight."

"*Ja*, that's *gut*." Levy rested his arms on the table. "It's the only thing we can do during times of trouble."

That night, after she put Mercy to sleep in her crib, Eliza lay in bed with her Bible on the pillow before her. The kerosene lamp flared in the gentle summer breeze through her open window.

She knew shunning was based on several passages of Scripture. She flipped to the eighteenth chapter of Matthew and read about how to deal with someone who sins. The first step was to "go and point out their fault, just between the two of you." If that didn't work, believers were instructed to escalate the issue by getting the testimony of witnesses, then tell the church, then shun them.

Shunning also was supported by numerous other passages. Eliza reviewed the portions recommending how disobedience is to be treated. Believers should have "no company" with the sinners, which should convince sinners to "be ashamed" of their behavior. A believer was to hold himself apart from the sinner so as to keep himself pure.

Technically—though she was a believer with all her heart—she wasn't part of the church. At the moment, that was her saving grace.

She closed her Bible, blew out the lamp and rolled over to stare at the black ceiling, wondering what "fault" she might have committed that would cause gossip among others at the Sabbath services, then prompt the bishop to want to speak to her.

The terror that drenched her at the thought of shunning made her realize how very much she wanted to be baptized. All uncertainty was gone. This was the right course of action—for Mercy, for herself...and for her soul.

Levy might warn her against assuming the

worst, but she couldn't help it. She had tried
so hard to be good, to regain respectability,
after her return to the church community. She
had worked hard, helping Levy and Jane with
their business. She had cared for her child. And
now… Was it too late to be baptized?

She cried herself to sleep.

Chapter Twelve

With enormous trepidation, Eliza walked beside Levy toward the bishop's residence. She knew he had an office in back where he met with church members.

"Don't be nervous, *liebling*," said Levy.

"Wouldn't you be?" she countered.

"Well, *ja*, I guess I would." He fell silent for a moment, then added, "But Bishop Kemp is a merciful man. Just don't let your temper run away with you and you'll be okay."

"Temper. My eternal flaw. It's what pulled me away from here." She sighed.

The bishop and his wife resided in a *daadi haus* in the back of his youngest son's farmhouse. Levy led the way toward the door.

"I'll wait out here," he told her, pointing to a bench in the shade of a tree. He leaned forward and kissed her on the forehead.

Eliza walked up to the door of the *daadi haus*. She drew a deep breath and knocked.

Edith Kemp, the bishop's wife, opened the door. "*Guder nammidaag*, Eliza. My husband is expecting you."

No polite chitchat, no social graces to smooth over the transition. Eliza wiped her hands on her apron and followed Edith into the house toward the back, where Bishop Kemp sat behind a plain desk in a sparse office.

"Ah, Eliza." He stood up and gestured toward a chair. "Please, be seated."

"*Danke.*" She pulled the chair a bit closer to the desk and sat down. "I'll confess your request to meet with you disturbed me," she said. "I don't know what I might have done to require it."

"Some reports have met my ears of an alarming nature," he replied. He rested his clasped hands on the desktop. "It concerns your relations with Josiah Lapp."

Eliza's jaw dropped. "My relations with Josiah? *What* relations with Josiah?"

"Are you seeing Josiah?"

"I see him nearly every day. He and his crew are doing some construction to the house. Levy and Jane are expecting a baby, as you know, and the house was never large to begin with."

Bishop Kemp flapped a hand with, she thought,

a touch of irritation. "That's not what I mean and you know it. Eliza, I'll be blunt. You had a reputation to overcome when you returned to our church community, and you've expressed an interest in being baptized. Now I wonder if that will work."

Hot anger threatened to swamp Eliza. How dare the bishop throw her past in her face? Mindful of Levy's advice to curb her temper, she strove to keep her voice level. "Bishop Kemp, I need to make one thing perfectly clear. The 'reputation' I overcame was simply the result of adolescent misjudgment. I should never have left the Amish, but I broke no vows in my decision to do so. I wasn't baptized. *Ja*, it's true I had a whirlwind romance with a wild *Englischer*, and it's true I regretted marrying him, but Mercy was born in lawful wedlock. After my husband died and after Mercy was born, I realized I couldn't raise her without help. That's why I sent her to Levy. Then I saw the error of my ways and returned home. And that, Bishop Kemp, should be the end of the story."

"But is it?" he countered calmly.

"*Ja*," she snapped. "It is. I have spent the last year walking the straight and narrow. Levy and Jane can testify to that."

He gave her a grave nod. "Their testimony will have to be considered, of course, but…"

Eliza felt herself grow pale. "Testimony for what? Of what am I being accused?"

"Eliza." Bishop Kemp steepled his fingers and leaned back in his chair. "Reports have reached me that you and Josiah are meeting in secret for…for unknown reasons. This, as you can imagine, reflects poorly on your reputation and makes me question whether you will ever be a suitable candidate for baptism."

Shock flattened her face, and she stared. "Secretly meeting… Bishop Kemp, I can assure you no such 'secret meetings' have ever occurred!"

"*Gut.* I'm glad to hear it. But that's your side of the story…"

"*Ja*, it's my side!" Red-hot anger flushed through her. "Bishop Kemp, since returning home, I've spent my time here abiding by the rules of the *Ordnung.* Aside from Mercy, my greatest earthly gift has been returning to the church. I don't know what kind of gossip you've been listening to, but the Bible says gossiping is a sin. But it seems you're listening to sinful gossip."

"Eliza, calm down…"

"I *won't* calm down," she snapped. "One of the things I discovered in the *Englisch* world is that people have the impression the Amish are a perfect and flawless group. Well, I'm flawed. I've owned up to it. I came crawling home to redeem myself. So why is the gossip falling on me? Am I just a convenient scapegoat for bad behavior because of my past faults?"

"Eliza, please. I would not say these things if I did not have concerns. I myself saw Josiah at your brother's place after the storm, when you were alone."

She remembered viewing the bishop on the road in his wagon that day. He must have noticed Josiah cleaning up for her.

"He was there to help! I was alone, *ja*, and the window broke…"

"There's more. Someone saw you two together on the road from a *youngie* event at dark. And then there is your contact with the *Englisch* man."

Her head spun as she thought of the many innocent encounters and conversations she'd had that were now being presented in a sinister way. She swallowed.

"My only contact with the *Englisch* man is to consider an offer for my dolls, which I sew to help support myself and pay my brother back for his help. As for talking to Josiah on the road…" She couldn't go on. Her throat clogged with frustration. Why should she have to defend these simple and harmless interactions?

To her frustration, she burst into tears. She jerked to her feet so fast she sent the chair flying backward to the floor. "Why are people spreading lies about me?" she sobbed. She whirled and yanked open the office door. She ran from the room, ran out of the *daadi haus*, ran through the sunny yard.

"Eliza!" Levy sprinted to catch up with her.

"Leave me alone," she wept. She shoved past him and walked as fast as she could away from Bishop Kemp's farm.

"I won't." He handed her a clean handkerchief. "Here, take this."

She groped for the cloth and buried her face in it. She stumbled, and he took her arm to steady her.

To her relief, he didn't probe about the cause of her distress. He simply walked beside her, with sturdy strides, as she sobbed into the handkerchief. She blessed her brother for his restraint.

She didn't offer any explanations on the way home. Not until she climbed onto the back porch, where Jane was doing laundry, did she say a word.

Jane turned and made an exclamation of distress when she saw Eliza. "What happened? Are you okay?"

Eliza sobbed harder. Levy directed her to a chair and sat her down. To Jane he replied, "I don't know yet what happened. She ran out of the bishop's house crying, and hasn't said a word all the way home."

Jane eased herself into a chair and reached out to touch Eliza's arm. "Come on, tell us what happened. You'll feel better for it."

Eliza hiccupped and gave a shuddering sigh. She mopped her eyes and blew her nose. "I'm sorry, it's like everything that's been building up in me just came out all at once."

"So the bishop had bad news, then?" Jane bit her lip.

"He—he…" Eliza hiccupped again and tried to control herself. "He told me reports had reached him that Josiah and I are secretly meeting for what he called 'unknown reasons.' The innuendo was clear. He s-said that kind of behavior reflects badly on my reputation and makes him question whether I'll ever be a suitable candidate for baptism. He'd even heard of the *Englischer* who wants to buy my dolls and wondered about that contact. It was too much. And—and I lost my temper."

"And what did *you* say?" Levy also sat down, and folded his arms on the table.

"I s-said he's been listening to sinful gossip, that the Bible says gossiping is a sin. Then I b-burst out crying and just ran away." She pounded a fist on the porch rail. "How could he accuse me of such things?"

"Oh, Eliza." Jane's face drew into lines of sympathy. "He obviously heard false information, but how could you lose your temper and insult the bishop? That's a grave breach of manners."

"I know. I know." She twisted the damp handkerchief. "But I just got so mad thinking about the viciousness of gossip and how much unfounded rumors can ruin someone. And I can take a guess who's behind this gossip."

"Who?" Jane looked bewildered.

"Ruby."

"Josiah's mother?"

"*Ja.* She hates me. She's never approved of anything I've done since returning home. Last week, after she watched Mercy for the day, it seemed like the ice was thawing and we might reach a truce. But then everything blew up yesterday at the Sabbath service."

"You don't know Ruby's behind it," said Levy.

She glared at him. "Whose side are you on?"

"I'm only saying there's no proof, and it's no better to slander and blame Ruby without evidence than it is for someone to slander your own reputation."

"But both she and Bishop Kemp said the same thing, questioning my suitability for baptism."

"Eliza…" he said on a warning note.

"All right, all right." She stared at the sodden handkerchief in her lap, her thoughts tumultuous and bitter. "But there sure seems to be a lot of hot gossip lately, and I wish I knew the source."

"We'll find it out soon enough." Jane cocked her head. "I think Mercy's awake. Why don't you go wash your face and I'll bring her down."

"Ja. Danke." Eliza stumbled to her feet and went to the kitchen sink to scrub away evidence of her hysteria.

By the time Jane reentered the kitchen with the sleepy toddler on her hip, Eliza's misery was receding and anger was taking its place—cold, calculating anger. Levy was right. She couldn't prove Ruby was the source of the rumors, but she vowed not to trust the older woman.

She also hoped to avoid seeing her again at all costs.

Levy returned to his work, and Eliza offered to relieve Jane from washing clothes. She was able to work out some of her temper with the swing-arm lever washer as she finished the load and fed the garments through the wringer.

"I'll hang them," Eliza offered. "Mercy, come with *Mamm, ja?*"

Walking slowly so the toddler could follow, Eliza went toward the backyard clothesline where she snapped a garment straight and pinned it to the line.

"Are you all right?"

She turned and saw Josiah, tool belt around his waist and sawdust clinging to his shirt. "Go away," she said crossly. "I don't feel like talking."

"What's happened?" he persisted.

She snapped straight another shirt and pinned it to the line with ruthless efficiency. "Josiah, I said I don't feel like talking."

"You *are* talking." He crossed his arms. "I get the impression this involves me, that's why I'm asking."

She whirled. "If you must know, I just had a very uncomfortable interview with Bishop Kemp, who more or less accused me of inappropriate behavior with you. *Now* will you leave me alone?"

His face flattened in shock. "Inappro… Eliza, what are you talking about?"

"*You* tell *me*. I'm just as much in the dark." She returned to her task.

"Why did he accuse you of such a thing?"

"My only guess is he's been listening to gossip." Mindful of Levy's warning about unfairly accusing someone, she refrained from mentioning his mother.

"Eliza, what gossip? I insist you tell me what you know, especially if this involves me."

"Fine." She turned to face him and crossed her arms. "Yesterday, if you remember, I was the recipient of a lot of hostile looks and whispered gossip at the Sabbath service. I didn't know the cause, but even you picked it up. Then yesterday afternoon, Bishop Kemp came over and asked if he could see me today. As you can imagine, I dreaded the worst, up to and including *meidung*."

She saw him flinch and grow pale. "He wouldn't…"

"I didn't know. That's the problem, I didn't know. So today when I met with him, he said he's heard reports that you and I were secretly meeting for what he called 'unknown reasons.' He didn't say what those reasons were, but the innuendo was obvious. He mentioned how you were here alone after the storm, and how we were seen together alone walking home from the *youngie* event. He also knew of the *Englischer*'s interest in my dolls. He said this reflects badly on my reputation and makes him question whether I'll ever be a suitable candidate for baptism." She thinned her lips. "Unfortunately I lost my temper and told him gossip is sinful, and he's been listening to gossip. Then I left. As you can imagine, I'm not in a very good mood right now. And that, Josiah, is why I don't feel like talking to you." She turned her back to him and continued hanging laundry.

"But I don't understand. Who would plant such ideas in the bishop's mind when you've done nothing wrong?"

She stopped herself from hurling his mother's name at him. Let him figure it out himself. He lived with her, after all. Instead she retorted, "Your ignorance is causing me a lot of problems, Josiah. It's time you made up your mind about some things." She clipped the last item to the clothesline, picked up the laundry basket in one arm and Mercy in the other and marched away.

Back in the house, she put Mercy down and looked out the kitchen window. Josiah stared at the ground, obviously in perplexed thought. After a few minutes, he wandered back toward the construction crew and continued his work.

Eliza turned away. She'd lost her temper again. When she was young, before she left the community, her temper would flare up with no warning, at the slightest provocation, big or small. In the *Englisch* world, where she didn't suppress her feelings, it had subsided, and she'd thought that was a sign she should stay out of the Amish community. Now she was back, and her temper was, too. When would she learn this was not an effective way to deal with a situation? She bit her lip and fought back tears.

Mercy lifted her arms up again. "*Mamm*, up!"

"*Liebling.*" She smiled at the child and swung her up. She felt her undergarment. "Clean diaper? *Gut* girl. Come help me sew some more dolls."

She brought her daughter into the partitioned area and set her down. "Can you pick out your favorite colors?" she asked, and placed a basket of scraps on the floor. Mercy sat down and pawed through the basket in an established game. Eliza seated herself at the treadle sewing machine and began assembling body parts for a new production run of dolls.

The business card from Christopher Morris, the wholesaler she'd talked to, rested on the table. She fed the doll parts through the needle and thought about him. She hadn't said yes or no to his offer, but now she seriously thought about what it might entail. Levy was right, she was selling too well now to consider making any extra dolls for a wholesaler, but what about winter and spring, when the farmers market was closed and she would have more time? Could she do it then?

Tears stung her eyes again as she realized what she was doing—again. She was thinking about leaving. About running away. About leaving her church community, leaving her support structure, taking her daughter and starting a new life somewhere else.

She didn't want to, but she could. This man, this wholesaler, might provide the means by which she could support herself and her baby. She could earn a precarious living on her own somewhere else. She wouldn't leave the Amish and return to the *Englisch* world, though. She'd experienced too much heartache along that path. To her mind, leaving the Amish was not an option.

But she could leave Grand Creek and settle with another Amish community farther away. That's what Jane did, after all, when she came here. Nothing prevented her from doing something similar. She could become baptized someplace else.

The grim thoughts continued to circle her mind as her fingers flew through the work in front of her.

Josiah was distracted the rest of the afternoon.

"Okay?" asked his foreman, clearly finishing up an explanation of something Josiah hadn't heard at all.

He blinked at the man standing before him. "I'm sorry, say that again?"

The other man sighed and launched again into his question. This time Josiah was able to follow.

He finished the afternoon's work efficiently but blindly, remembering little beyond Eliza's anger at her interview with the bishop.

Your ignorance is causing me a lot of problems... It's time you made up your mind about some things...

Eliza's words haunted him. Of what was he ignorant?

He shook his head and allowed annoyance to come to the forefront. Women. Sometimes he thought he should follow the example of one of his uncles who had never married. The older man lived in bachelor splendor in the *daadi haus* behind his sister's family, Josiah's aunt. Maybe he was onto something by never marrying and never immersing himself in the complicated emotions that seemed to come naturally to women.

At the end of the workday, he thanked his crew, removed his tool belt, ran a bandanna over his forehead and headed for home.

"I have a casserole ready for you, *lieb*," his mother told him once he entered the kitchen.

"Ja, danke." Josiah washed his hands and seated himself at the kitchen table. After the silent blessing, he tackled the subject head-on.

"*Mamm*, Eliza had a meeting with the bishop this afternoon," he began.

His mother's fork suspended midair. "*Ja?*" she inquired. "What about?"

"About some gossip that's damaging her reputation."

"Gossip." Ruby finished her bite. "*Ja*, I can imagine there's a lot of gossip about her."

"Gossip has to start somewhere. And this time the gossip included me." He leveled a stern glance at his mother. "Do you know how this gossip started?"

"No." Ruby looked down at her plate. "How would I know how such a thing started?"

"Because you were one of the people passing it around yesterday at the Sabbath meeting."

"Josiah! How dare you accuse me of such a thing?"

"I'm stating a fact. I saw you whispering with other women and glaring at Eliza."

"Nobody needs to whisper anything when it's clear as day who she is. Even you said she's getting involved with *Englisch* again."

"*Mamm*, you know that is for her business! I told you that!" The fact that his mother would twist his example of Eliza's industriousness into something negative made his stomach burn and his suspicions grow.

"You seem to care a lot for what Eliza says and does."

"I already told you why, but that's not the issue here. The issue is gossip. The bishop told her she and I have been secretly meeting for 'unknown reasons.' That's untrue, but now everyone thinks that. Now this vicious gossip is ruining my own reputation. Don't you care about that?"

"Of course I care. But it shows what happens when you express an interest in a woman with a reputation like Eliza's."

"And what reputation is that?"

Ruby toyed with her food and didn't answer.

"*Mamm*, I want to know what you think Eliza is like," persisted Josiah. "Because I suspect whatever you think is wrong."

"She left," blurted Ruby. "She left the church community."

"*Ja*, and she wasn't the first. Many do, during their *rumspringa*. And then they come back, just as she did. She wasn't baptized at the time, so she broke no vows. And she's behaved well since she returned."

"Has she? Has she really behaved well?"

"What have you heard that makes you think she hasn't?"

Ruby flapped a hand. "Lots of things…"

"That won't do, *Mamm*, and you know it.

Give me specifics. What have you heard that makes you think she hasn't behaved well? Because if something damaging but untrue is circulating, she needs to know it so she can defend herself."

"What do you care?" burst Ruby. "She's not worth your interest!"

Josiah clamped down on his temper. His mother's obsession over Eliza's shortcoming was disturbing. What was going on here?

He kept his voice calm. "In the end, *Mamm*, my interest in Eliza isn't your business. You have no say in who I do or do not court. But what *is* my business is that harmful gossip that may disturb my standing in the community. Let me remind you I've been supporting you since *Daed* passed away. That's my duty as your youngest son, and one I take seriously since you sacrificed so much to raise us all. But what happens if my business fails because people believe the false gossip that I'm doing something nefarious with Eliza? Can't you see how that kind of gossip can have long-range ramifications?"

His mother looked stricken. "I… I…"

"So you *didn't* see." He nodded. His mother had been traumatized by the loss of her husband, he knew. He knew he was being tough, and he hated being tough with his own mother, but she needed to understand that her actions mattered now that she was widowed.

He softened his words by patting her hand as it lay idle on the table. "*Mamm*, I love you. But please, don't make things harder on me by trying to influence my personal life." He gave her a sad smile. "Meanwhile, let me ask you something. Have you considered seeing a grief counselor about handling *Daed*'s passing?"

Ruby frowned and looked down at her plate. "That's not necessary."

"I know using an *Englisch* counselor isn't common, but it might help you. Grief is universal, even among the *Englisch*."

"I don't want to talk about it." Ruby clamped her mouth shut.

"Fine. You don't have to *talk* about it. But please, *think* about it."

Whatever his mother's issue with Eliza, her longstanding sorrow over the loss of her husband might well be behind a lot of her personal problems. Josiah hoped she would take his suggestion seriously.

Chapter Thirteen

Heavy-eyed, Eliza dragged herself out of bed the next morning and attended to Mercy's needs.

"You look awful," remarked Jane in sisterly sympathy as Eliza carried the toddler downstairs and into the kitchen.

"Didn't sleep well." Eliza slipped the baby into her high chair and knuckled her eyes. "But work must go on. Levy said the blueberries are starting to peak, so I'll pick some this morning and work on blueberry jam later today for selling at Saturday's market. But I do need to go to your aunt and uncle's store this morning—they were expecting a shipment of fabric in for me and I'll need it. I can take the wagon to bring it home."

"And I'll watch this little *boppli*." Jane chucked Mercy under the chin with affection.

Josiah and his crew arrived to work on the

house, but Eliza avoided any possible interaction with him. She did catch a glimpse of his face, looking as drawn and preoccupied as she imagined hers looked.

In the late morning, with two gallons of blueberries in the kitchen waiting to be turned into jam, Eliza washed her face and hands, pinned on a fresh apron and kissed her daughter goodbye.

"Do you need anything at the store?" she asked Jane.

"No, I'm fine. I'm glad you're getting out," said Jane. "You've been working double duty and now this extra burden is on you. Take your time and enjoy the walk."

"Danke." She smiled at her sister-in-law, once again thanking *Gott* He had sent such a wonderful woman for her brother to marry.

The day was lovely, with puffy clouds overhead. Not too hot, not too humid, and birds sang along the edges of the gravel road as Eliza pulled the wagon behind her. Jane was right. It was good to get out. She felt some of her worries start to recede.

The center of town, consisting of narrow crossroads, loomed ahead. Eliza pulled the wagon up the wooden ramp to the broad porch outside the Troyers' dry goods store. She left the wagon and turned to enter the store when another woman exited. Eliza almost bumped into the last person she wanted to see—Ruby Lapp.

"*Guder mariye*, Ruby." Eliza kept her voice polite.

Ruby looked dismayed. Her expression altered from civil to hostile. "Get out of my way," the older woman growled. "I don't want to see you."

Eliza had not survived four years and myriad dire experiences in the wider world to be bullied on a quiet store porch. "That makes two of us, Ruby, but all I said was 'Good morning.' I'm sorry you can't be civil back."

"Why are you here?"

Eliza raised her eyebrows and she spoke with dignity. "I'm picking up some fabric. I have a business now, Ruby. I'm making dolls to sell. It's helping me be financially independent. That means I don't have to marry anyone—anyone at all—to support myself and my baby."

"Eliza Struder, I'll thank you to stay away from my son." Ruby spoke in a steely voice. "He's going to be courting someone else and you have no right to interfere."

"I'm don't care who he courts because it's none of my business," replied Eliza. She kept her voice firm and calm, but inside she was seething. How dare Ruby make untrue accusations in a public place? "But it's also high time you stop blaming me for whatever is happening in your son's private life. If you have an issue with something he's said or done, why don't you take it up with him, rather than berate an innocent third party?"

Scarlet color surged into Ruby's cheeks. "Innocent third party?" she spat. "I don't think so. My son was doing fine until you came back."

Eliza crossed her arms. "And he is doing fine now, for all I know. It's none of my business."

"I have eyes. I can see what you're doing."

"And what am I doing?"

The other woman worked her mouth, but no words came out. She glared.

"I insist you tell me what it is you think I'm doing," pursued Eliza. She kept her voice calm and controlled. "Because someone around here is spreading untrue gossip about me, and I would certainly appreciate knowing just what, precisely, I'm accused of. Or do you even know?"

Dimly, from inside the store, she saw a shadowy figure near the open window, listening to the altercation.

Ruby snapped her mouth shut. Then she gathered herself and said, "Your reputation precedes you, Eliza, and I can see you've learned nothing about humility and decency. This is why I've been against your baptism."

Hot fury washed over Eliza, but she knew if

she lost her temper, she would lose all standing in Ruby's eyes. "My reputation, as you call it, has been impeccable since I returned to the community. I challenge you to pinpoint anything, anything at all, that goes against the *Ordnung*."

"You know what you've done!" shrilled Ruby. "I don't need to fill you in on your own bad behavior!"

The store's front door whipped open and Catherine Troyer stepped outside. "Ruby," she said. "Please, this is not the place for a private argument. I must ask you to be more respectful while on our property."

"Even against this *trollop*?" Ruby spat the word.

Eliza gasped. Catherine gasped.

Ruby looked from one face to the other, and her own expression crumpled. "I'm sorry," she mumbled. "I didn't mean to say that. I'll leave now."

Catherine moved toward Ruby and put a sympathetic arm around the older woman's shoulders. "Now, now," she soothed. "I know you've had a hard time since your husband died, but there's no need to project your grief on anyone else. Can I make you a cup of tea?"

"No." Ruby shook off Catherine's arm and turned to face Eliza. "I apologize," she repeated.

"I didn't mean to say that. It—it just came out." She sniffed. "I'll be going now."

Eliza watched Ruby walk down the porch steps and away from the center of town.

Catherine spoke quietly, her gaze on the retreating figure. "Something is eating her up inside, and it has nothing to do with you."

The reaction from the altercation caught up with Eliza, and she started trembling. Tears spilled from her eyes. "I don't understand what's happening," she sniffled. "Why is everyone suddenly against me? I've tried so hard to fit back into the church community. I want nothing more than to stay here and raise Mercy. I don't understand why all this hostility is suddenly everywhere…"

Catherine drew her into the store. "I'll make tea," she repeated. "But for you, not Ruby. Come in back, it's quiet there."

Shoulders bowed, Eliza followed the motherly woman toward the back of the store, where some domestic comforts were set up, including a propane burner and beverage accoutrements.

Catherine gently pushed Eliza toward a padded chair. Eliza collapsed into it and fished her handkerchief out of her pocket to mop her eyes.

"Now." Catherine poured water into a kettle and set it on the gas ring. "Tell me what that was all about."

"I wish I knew." Eliza sniffled. "Something's going on around me, and I don't know what it is."

"What do you mean, something's going on around you?"

"You were at the Sabbath meeting two days ago, weren't you?"

"*Ja*, of course."

"Did you pick up any of the whispered gossip that was happening everywhere I looked?"

Catherine spooned a bit of sugar into two mugs. "I saw groups gathered together talking, but that happens every week. I didn't hear any gossip against you. But since my connection to you is well-known through Jane and Levy, probably I was excluded from hearing it. For which," she added, "I'm grateful. Gossip is evil and a sin."

"*Ja*, I know. But what happened…" Eliza pleated the handkerchief in agitation. "Well, actually, let me go back a bit further. Saturday before last, when Jane was still in the hospital, she and Levy were fretting about missing the farmers market. Even missing one weekend would mean losing a good chunk of income for them."

"But you did the market in their place, *ja*?"

"*Ja*, both Josiah and I did. We both worked it together. Ruby watched Mercy, and everything seemed to go so well. I was relieved there was a—a kind of cease-fire of hostilities with her."

"So what happened?"

"I wish I knew. Day before yesterday, it came roaring back, and it seemed everyone was whispering about me. Then Sunday afternoon, Bishop Kemp came to the house and asked to speak to me the next day."

"The bishop asked to speak to you?" Catherine stared, her hands suspended over the tea things.

"*Ja.* Yesterday, when we met, he expressed doubts about whether I would be a suitable candidate for baptism."

"*Gott* have mercy." Catherine dropped into a nearby chair. "Why would he say such a thing?"

"Because he was listening to *gossip.*" Eliza nearly spat the word. "I—I'm afraid I lost my temper with him." Fresh tears welled up. "I know that wasn't right, but I've been on a trigger's edge lately with all these bad feelings swirling around me, especially since I don't know why they started. So anyway, now Ruby is very angry with me, and again I don't know why." She sniffed.

Catherine rose from her seat and poured the hot water into mugs. She handed Eliza the beverage, along with a spoon. "I wonder..." she mused.

"Wonder what?" probed Eliza, when Catherine seemed disinclined to continue.

"I wonder about Ruby. She's had such a hard time adjusting since her husband died. Harder than most. But there's something deeper here, something that makes me think…" Catherine's expression turned inward, as if searching a memory.

"Whatever it is, I resent her taking it out on me." Eliza stopped and pinched the bridge of her nose. "I'm sorry, that sounded petty and unforgiving."

"You're rattled. I understand." Catherine's gaze was soft with compassion. The older woman sighed. "The sins of the past," she murmured.

Eliza's attention sharpened. She remembered the warning Catherine had given her weeks ago at the *youngie* hot dog roast, when Catherine had alluded to her own rebellious youth. *A number of us older women have something in our past we're ashamed of. Remember that*, she'd said.

But until now, she'd forgotten.

"Could Ruby have something in her past she's ashamed of?" she mused, then realized too late she'd spoken the words out loud.

Catherine did not reply, but she smiled over her teacup.

Sensing she was on the right course, Eliza continued to ponder out loud, "My understanding is Ruby has led a quiet life since her husband died. She's not doing anything outside the *Ordnung*. She's like a good, solid member of the community and no scandal has ever touched her. Whereas I'm nothing *but* scandal." Her words held weary acceptance.

Catherine nodded. "I think you have less scandal than you think. Or to put it another way, you're manufacturing more scandal in your background than you actually experienced. I know it's hard to see now, but there will come a point in your life where the hardship you experienced will become a valuable teaching tool for someone else. You might find yourself counseling a rebellious *youngie* at some point in the future." She paused. "After all, that's what *I'm* doing, *ja*?"

Catching the humor, Eliza smiled and felt better. She remembered Catherine's confession about her own youthful proclivities. "*Ja, Gott* willing." She drained her tea. "One thing is certain," she concluded. "Your niece has become my sister in every possible way. I couldn't love her more than if she was of my own blood, and I thank *Gott* every day Levy married her."

"*Ja*, that's *gut*, then." Catherine rose. "Remember, this too shall pass. Come now, I have some beautiful bolts of fabric for your doll-making."

Catherine's common-sense analysis buoyed Eliza on the walk home. Pulling the wagon loaded with bolts of fabric, thread and bags of stuffing, she reflected how Catherine's own somewhat shady past was, indeed, serving as a teaching tool for her own difficulties. She wondered if someday she would be called to pay it forward.

Pay it forward. She paused and remembered the advice of the kindly pastor and his wife who had paid for her return to the community. The only repayment they wanted was for her to look for an opportunity to pay the kindness forward to someone else who might need it.

That opportunity certainly hadn't arisen yet. It was a debt Eliza would gladly repay; yet it seemed her life since returning to her home community had become more complicated than she anticipated. How would she ever be in a position to pay anything forward?

She sighed and prayed for patience and forbearance. *This too shall pass*, Catherine had said. Those were wise words indeed.

When she arrived home, she kept her dispute with Ruby to herself and didn't mention anything to her sister-in-law.

"That's beautiful," commented Jane, fingering the bright bolts of cotton Eliza unloaded from the wagon.

"*Ja*, I think so, too. I'm making so many dolls that I'll probably have most of this gone within a month."

"Speaking of which, if you want to get some sewing done, I'll keep an eye on Mercy. She can help me pick more blueberries for jam."

"Are you feeling up for it?"

"*Ja*. Picking isn't hard work, it just takes a while. And I wouldn't mind getting outdoors, since it's such a pretty day. Not too hot."

"What do you think, *liebling*?" Eliza picked up her daughter and cuddled her. "Do you want to pick blueberries with Aunt Jane?"

"Boo-biss," burbled the toddler, and Eliza laughed. Whatever personal difficulties she was experiencing, she knew Mercy was in the best possible place to grow up.

With Mercy under supervision outside, Eliza settled into her sewing station and began working on dolls. The usual clamor of hammers and saws rang outside the house, but she was used to it by now.

"Have you seen Levy?"

She looked up and saw Josiah. Her heart thudded, as it always did when seeing him. But this time she was still smarting from the encounter with his mother.

"He's out in the barn, I think." She snipped a thread. "Josiah, I want a word with you. Can you please ask your mother to leave me alone?"

"What?" He stared at her. "What are you talking about? Where did this come from?"

"I just returned from a trip to the Troyers' store to pick up some fabric. I bumped into your mother, and she spent a fair bit of time insulting me."

"*Insulting* you?" He removed his hat and wiped some sweat from his forehead. "That doesn't sound like her."

"Well, be surprised, then. Catherine Troyer witnessed it, so I'm not making this up. I know your mother doesn't like me, and that's fine, but she has no right to accost me on the sidewalk and spit names in my face."

His expression hardened from bafflement to annoyance. "She most certainly does not. I apologize on her behalf, Eliza. Whatever her problem is, she has no right to take it out on you."

"*Danke.*" She focused on the fabric beneath her fingers. "I realize you're in a tough position, Josiah, and I apologize for bringing this up. But at some point her behavior is going to start catching up with her and reflect worse on her than on me."

"Why would *her* behavior reflect on *you*?"

"Because of what she's accusing me of doing. Or being."

"What is she accusing you of?"

"I don't really want to get into that now." Ruby's words still stung. "I just know she was out of line." She jerked her head toward the doorway. "As I said, Levy's in the barn. Now excuse me, I have some sewing to do." She turned away.

After a moment Josiah left, but Eliza's hands paused over her work.

Maybe she *should* leave the community. She hated being the subject of gossip, and it seemed too many people couldn't overlook the baggage of the poor decisions she made when younger. As Mercy grew up, she didn't want her precious baby to be on the receiving end of any gossip, either.

A clean, fresh start held some attraction. She now had a means of earning a living on her own. It broke her heart to think of leaving her beloved brother and sister-in-law, but in light of how much trouble she'd been having settling back into the community, perhaps this was *Gott*'s way of telling her she shouldn't be baptized. Or at least, not baptized here in Grand Creek.

Chapter Fourteen

"Are you sure you feel up to going?" Eliza handed Jane a large basket containing wrapped batches of cookies.

"*Ja*. Don't fuss so, *liebling*. I feel fine. Fine and strong." Jane hefted the basket into her arms while Eliza picked up a heavier box of dolls. "It's funny, I find I miss doing the farmers market now that I've taken a couple weeks off from it. Maybe some of Levy's salesmanship is rubbing off on me."

Eliza followed Jane out into the cool morning air. The sun had barely risen. "Well, if you're sure…"

"I'm sure. Besides, someone I could mention isn't going to let me overdo it." With a twinkle in her eyes, she handed the basket up to Levy, who stood in the back of the wagon arranging crates and boxes of produce.

"You can bet I won't." Levy smiled down at his wife, then winked at his sister.

Eliza laughed. The change in her brother since marrying Jane still amazed her. Once a serious young man, burdened with raising his little sister at too young an age after their parents died, Levy now showed a side of himself Eliza had never seen—humor, strength and a devoted love whenever he looked at the ordinary woman with glasses whose plain features became almost beautiful whenever she smiled at her husband.

She waved at the departing wagon loaded to the brim with goods to sell at the market, then turned back toward the house. The day loomed before her, quiet and peaceful. No carpentry work outside, no brother or sister-in-law in the kitchen. With Mercy still asleep, Eliza intended to get a jump start on her next production run of dolls.

She got two solid hours of work done before she heard her daughter wail from her crib. She hurried upstairs to lift up the sleepy toddler. "Now, now, *liebling. Mamm* is here. Do you need your diaper changed? Yes, you do, then I have a wonderful blueberry muffin for you for breakfast. Would you like that?"

As was her custom, Eliza changed the child's diaper, then spent a few minutes rocking with her until her daughter fully woke up. Feeling the small head pressed against her in such a trusting manner never ceased filling her with maternal love for the baby.

"Hun-gy," said Mercy, pulling herself upright.

"Me, too. Your aunt Jane made some muffins for breakfast. *Komm*, let's go find them."

She picked up the child and brought her downstairs into the kitchen. In a few moments, Mercy was happily sitting in her high chair, gumming on a muffin.

The morning passed. She brought Mercy outside and suffered through the child's "help" while picking some more blueberries. She took a basket and showed Mercy where to find eggs for gathering in the chicken yard. She and the toddler picked green beans for that evening's dinner.

By the time early afternoon came, the toddler was heavy-eyed and ready for her nap. Eliza laid her down and returned to her sewing.

A few minutes later, she heard a knock at the front door. Leaving her work, she padded over and opened it. Josiah stood on the porch.

Her heart zoomed into her throat.

He was clean for once, not layered with sweat and sawdust that was the natural result of his hard carpentry work.

"Hello, Eliza," he said. "May I speak to you?"

"Levy and Jane aren't here," she felt compelled to inform him.

"*Ja*, I know. That's why I came."

She felt wary and trapped. What could he possibly have to say to her in the absence of her family? Especially when he knew people might notice? "*Ja*, come in." She knew her voice sounded less than inviting. Peering beyond him to see if any gossiping people were around, she stepped aside and allowed him to pass through the door.

Once inside, he acted nervous. He removed his straw hat and ran the brim through his fingers.

"Where's Mercy?" he finally asked.

"She's upstairs, napping." Eliza slipped her hands in her skirt pockets so their trembling wouldn't be obvious. "Josiah, what can I do for you? Why are you here?"

"I need to talk to you." He gestured toward the chairs. "Please, won't you sit?"

She lowered herself into the rocking chair while he sank into Levy's favorite seat. She stayed silent as he stared for a few moments at the hat in his hand.

Then he raised his eyes to hers. "I worry about you with this doll business of yours. It scares me to think you might drift back toward the *Englisch* world, even though it cost you so much heartache."

Whatever Eliza expected, it wasn't this. She stared at him. "Josiah, have I ever given you reason to think I was drifting back toward the *Englisch* world?" Her conscience pricked even as she said the words, since she'd been thinking of leaving the community and starting fresh somewhere else. Not among the *Englisch*, though…

As if reading her mind, Josiah fixed his eyes on her. "Have you?" he asked. "Have you ever wanted to go back?"

She met his gaze. "No." It was true. She'd been thinking of settling in another Amish community, not an *Englisch* one. "As for the doll business, all I'm trying to do is earn enough money to support me, and also Mercy."

"You wouldn't have to keep sewing if you married me," he blurted. "I love you, Eliza."

Her jaw dropped. A sense of sickening dread crept down her spine, bringing chills with it. After the week she'd had, accused by the bishop, confronting Ruby, this out-of-the-blue confession felt wrong. Terribly wrong.

"Eliza?" he prompted. "Did you hear me?"

She snapped her mouth shut. "*Ja*, I heard you. I'm just trying to think what to say."

"Say you love me back." A ghost of a smile hovered at the corners of his mouth.

"What *gut* is it if I do?" She jerked to her feet and started pacing the room. She whirled on him. "Josiah, you can't be in love with me. You can't."

"Why not?" He, too, rose from the chair. His hat fell to the floor with a soft thud. "I think I've always loved you, even before you left the community years ago. The other women I've dated, they were a balm to my ego, a way to convince myself I was wrong for wanting a woman who had left the church."

"And that's the very reason you can't marry me." She drew herself up tight and narrow. "I'm not baptized. I have too much baggage. Even the bishop thinks so. If you married me, Josiah, you would never have as much respect in the community. You would be subject to endless gossip and speculation. Just like I am. You would be saddled with a child who isn't yours." She bit her lip. "I'm not worth it."

"Let me be the judge of that."

"No, you *can't* be the judge of that." She wiped sweaty palms down the front of her apron. "Josiah, there's too much at stake. Your mother, for one. She would never accept me. You're her youngest son, it's up to you to take care of her in her widowhood. She wants you to marry anyone else, as long as it's not me.

How would she react if you suddenly told her we were getting married?"

He scowled. "It's my life."

"*Ja*, but we each have obligations outside ourselves. You have your mother. I have my daughter. Their needs must be considered."

"For Mercy, of course. She's just a baby. But my mother is different. I will still take care of her, but she has to accept that I'm a grown man and must make up my own mind."

"Have you told your mother your plans?"

"No…"

"You see? You don't want to hurt her. I understand that. She's your mother, after all, and the only parent you have left." She shook her head. "Marrying me is a bad idea, Josiah. There's too much at stake. We both have people in our lives we can't hurt."

"But you haven't told me yet whether you love me back."

Her face became drawn and she turned away. "You know I do. I've felt that way for a long time."

"Then that's all that matters. I'm willing to throw caution to the wind."

"Well, I'm not!" She whirled on him. "Don't you see? That's what I did when I was a teenager. I threw caution to the wind and left the church, left the community. I didn't think about the repercussions or how much I hurt the people I left behind. I wanted to follow my own selfish desires. The result was far worse than I could ever imagine. If my husband, Mercy's father, hadn't died when he had, I would be trapped in a loveless marriage with an unkind man."

"But if we got married, ours wouldn't be a loveless marriage!" he protested.

"For how long? How long could we be in love if everyone around us is against us? How long before love turned to hate? And then we'd be trapped." She shook her head. "No, Josiah. I'm not willing to go down that path again, much less drag along the man I love. You're in a position to keep your good name untarnished. But if you start courting me, then every past sin anyone thinks I've committed comes down on your head, as well. And a year from now you'll wake up and realize you made a terrible, terrible mistake."

"You're determined to look at the darkest side possible." He glowered and crossed his arms on his chest.

"Why shouldn't I look on the dark side? I've lived through darkness. I was just beginning to emerge into the light after coming home, but I know how fast things can go from light to dark."

"So you would have me marry someone else? Someone I don't love?"

"Of course not. Marry, or don't marry. That's your business. But don't do anything on account of me."

"I think you're overdramatizing everything, Eliza. People think well of you. Except my mother, that is."

"And the bishop. And all the gossiping women who threw me dark looks at the last Sabbath service. Is that what you want for your future, Josiah? Because I can assure you, no matter how perfectly I behave, people will always imagine the worst about me. If you associate with me, they'll imagine the worst about you, too. And if we get married, they'll assume the gossip is true."

"But why should they assume that? We've done nothing wrong."

She palmed a hand over her face in weariness. "Don't you remember what I told you the bishop said to me? He said he'd heard we were meeting in secret for 'unknown reasons.' You know exactly what people are thinking. If you suddenly start to court me, it just confirms those rumors."

He scowled. "That's not fair. None of it is true."

"*Ja*, tell me about it. However those rumors started…" She refrained from pinning any blame on his mother. "…they're out there and influencing peoples' thoughts and opinions. I've had a long time to get used to and accept that I'll always have a stain on my reputation, no matter how unfair that is. You don't, and I don't want you tainted by the sins people see in me."

"What sins?" he burst out in frustration. "You act as if no one has ever left the church during their *rumspringa* and then returned. Everyone knows you married and had a child. That is not a horrible crime."

"Then why doesn't your mother like me?" she retorted with heat. "It's a natural thing for people to assume the worst of someone, and that's the reputation I have to live down. I can only pray it won't affect Mercy when she's old enough to understand."

"So you're determined to rob me of any future happiness, then." He turned away, his face shuttered.

"No, I'm determined to *save* you from future unhappiness," she replied. "If you don't want to marry anyone else, fine. That's your choice. But marrying me would only bring on a world of hurt for both of us. I won't have it."

"This whole conversation didn't go anything like I'd planned."

Her anger departed, leaving sadness. "What did you expect?" she said. "That I would fall into your arms in everlasting devotion?"

"The thought had occurred to me." He turned to face her, and she was relieved to see the faintest glimmer of humor in his eyes.

"Give me up," she said quietly. "Find someone else to marry. In the end, you'll be glad you did."

He bent and picked up his straw hat, once again running the brim through his fingers in a gesture of agitation. Then he plopped the hat on his head.

"I won't ask you again," he said. "But my feelings haven't changed." He turned and walked out the door.

Eliza stared after him. Why oh why did he have to come through and disrupt her hard-won equilibrium? She wanted nothing more than to do what she had scoffed at—throw herself into his arms and declare her everlasting devotion.

Instead, she watched the man she loved walk away, both physically and metaphorically.

She sat down before the sewing machine and stared at her doll projects with hot eyes. Once again she thought about leaving. Not leaving the Amish, but leaving town.

To the side of the sewing machine was the business card of Christopher Morris, the wholesaler who wanted to carry her dolls. She picked it up and looked at it. She might be able to support herself if she agreed to sell her dolls to him. It would allow her the chance to settle elsewhere, maybe even in a different state.

On the card was Mr. Morris's phone number. She would need to go into town to find a telephone to use, but then she could speak with him and learn how many items he would want her to supply for wholesale orders. Suddenly she had a sense of urgency about this. She *must* look for a way to support herself and Mercy. If sewing dolls was the path to independence, then she would do it.

She would ask Levy to drive her into town on Monday. Or perhaps she could drive herself. She needed to find a telephone and speak to Mr. Morris—the sooner the better.

She laid down the business card and tackled her sewing once more, her thoughts chaotic. Mechanically she pumped the sewing machine's treadle and fed the fabric through the needle, wondering what it would be like to start afresh in a new community. Could she sacrifice her ties here for the sake of Josiah's good name?

She would be leaving behind Levy and Jane. Momentary grief clutched her heart at the thought. She loved her brother, and she loved her sister-in-law. She didn't know how she would have gotten through her return and subsequent adjustment to the community without them.

From upstairs, she heard Mercy give a wail

as she woke from her nap. Glad for an excuse to leave behind her grim thoughts, she went to soothe the baby and change her diaper. Then she sat down and rocked until the child was comforted.

"Are you hungry, *liebling*?"

"*Ja*. Mffn?"

"Muffin? You want another blueberry muffin?"

"*Ja.*" The toddler crammed a fist into her mouth.

"Let's go find one." She carried Mercy down into the kitchen and seated her in the high chair. "Here you go, *liebling*." She broke the muffin into pieces, and Mercy began to eat.

Watching her child, so content, made Eliza blink back tears. Could she rip Mercy away from this place, from these valuable family connections she herself now cherished? She knew only too well how vulnerable it was to be alone and friendless in a cold world. Of course, if she settled into another Amish community, she would not be without friends for long, and Mercy would grow up as comfortable there as here.

Her thoughts continued to whirl as she began preparing dinner for when Levy and Jane returned from the farmers market.

By the time she heard the familiar sound of

the horse's hooves clip-clopping up the drive-way two hours later, she'd made her plans. The first step was to talk to Christopher Morris, the wholesaler, and for that she needed to go into town. She composed her features into unassuming neutrality and vowed to say nothing about her interview with Josiah.

"Your uncle Levy and aunt Jane are home," she told her child, whose face lit up. She hoisted Mercy up on her hip and went to stand in the kitchen doorway, watching the wagon pull into the driveway toward the barn in back of the house.

Jane waved from the wagon seat. "Good sales today!" she called.

Levy paused the horse to allow Jane to climb down, then he directed the animal into the barn so he could unhitch and unload.

"How are you feeling?" inquired Eliza. "Tired? No, *liebling*, let Aunt Jane come inside first," she said as the toddler lifted her arms toward her aunt.

Jane laughed and took the toddler anyway, kissing the child's soft cheek. "I'm feeling wonderful. Levy hardly would let me stand or walk around until he realized sitting still just isn't in my nature," she chattered. "But I sat down whenever I needed to get off my feet. We sold every last one of your dolls and all the blueberry jam. We did very well on the vegetables and only have a little sweet corn left. Oh, and the wholesaler was back. He wanted to talk to you and seemed a bit disappointed to see me instead." She grinned.

Eliza nodded. "Actually, I wanted to talk to Levy about going into town on Monday so I can use a telephone. I want to discuss things with the wholesaler and see about him taking me on as a customer."

"I thought you might." Jane slid the toddler down to the floor. "Dinner smells *gut.*"

Levy came inside, swung Mercy around in a circle, then went to wash up while Eliza got their meal on the table. During the silent blessing, Eliza prayed for guidance as she prepared to lay her plans before her brother.

"Hmm, no, I don't think I can spare the time to take you into town," said Levy, talking with his mouth full. "But I'll hitch up the horse and you can drive yourself. I wouldn't mind if you could pick up a few items for me anyway, and I can tell you where there's a public telephone you can use to call him. But I thought you were going to wait until things slowed down in the winter before talking to him?"

"I've been thinking over my schedule," prevaricated Eliza. "I'm getting faster at making the dolls since I keep discovering efficient shortcuts. I want to talk to the wholesaler about numbers, how many dolls he wants me to supply him with. I want to see if I can handle the numbers he might give me. That will help me plan things out better."

She gave no hint about the possibility of leaving the community. That was a bigger subject than she wanted to tackle at the moment. Nothing was firmed up. She was doing only the preliminary legwork, she told herself.

Besides, she didn't want to distress Jane at the thought of moving away. Jane looked so content and happy at the moment—resting after a busy day, telling anecdotes about the customers they saw, pleased with how well sales went. Eliza didn't want to shatter her sister-in-law's peace of mind, so she kept a look of interest on her face and made no mention of her internal woes.

It wasn't until bedtime when she had the leisure to more fully probe the enormity of what she was contemplating. Nearby, Mercy breathed softly in her crib, slumbering.

The thought of leaving her hometown again had her feeling inconsolable. But could she stay, tortured by the nearness of Josiah while knowing she could not drag him down by marrying him? She rolled over and punched her pillow into a different shape. Could she continue to weather the gossip and the slurs upon her reputation? Could she subject Mercy to the baggage of her mother's past?

In many ways, leaving for another community might be the easiest solution, even if it was the most painful. She could begin afresh. She could raise Mercy amid a new circle of people. Perhaps she might even meet a nice man who didn't care about her history and whose mother would accept her.

The very thought of marrying anyone—anyone except Josiah—appalled her. That might be another complication she had to face—the thought that she might never marry at all.

But leave? She could do that. Maybe *Gott* was telling her what to do. And she had promised to always listen to what *Gott* told her.

Tears leaked onto the pillow below her restless head. If she thought returning home after her disastrous excursion into the *Englisch* world would solve all her problems, she was wrong. Absolutely wrong.

Chapter Fifteen

❧

Early Monday afternoon, Eliza climbed into the buggy seat behind Levy's favorite mare. The weather was blustery, with a hint of the autumn to come.

"I hope the phone call goes well," her brother told her. He gave the mare an affectionate pat on the rump. "We'll be curious what he says. Take your time. Jane is fine with watching Mercy as long as you need. Oh, but she wants to know if you could pick her up a few lemons while you're in town."

"*Ja*, I will. And I have your list of what you want at the hardware store." She touched her pocket, where she'd tucked both his list and the wholesaler's business card. "I also have a pen and notebook to write down what the wholesaler says." She braced the items on the seat beside her so they wouldn't blow away.

"See you in a couple hours, then." He stood aside, and Eliza guided the horse down the driveway.

She seldom drove a buggy by herself, and enjoyed the feeling of independence. An unaccompanied trip to town was fun and unusual, and she thought she might even treat herself to tea at a small coffee shop she knew about.

But business first. Her elation at the excursion faded as she considered what Mr. Morris might say. So far her doll business was a solo enterprise, and she didn't know what it would entail to bring into consideration the needs of a wider market. Her biggest concern was whether she could keep up with the increased demand.

Could she partner up with another woman with excellent sewing skills? She pondered the problem as the horse's hooves clip-clopped on the pavement. Not many women with suitable proficiency were free to tackle a sideline business—they were busy raising children. An older woman, perhaps? But most older women would not be interested in partnering with a younger boss.

The problem was unresolved by the time Eliza guided the horse through the town's traffic toward the public phone booth Levy mentioned, one of two or three the town kept for use by its Amish population. Eliza pulled the mare to a stop near a wide shady tree arcing over a hitching post. The breeze whisked the branches and made the shade dapple.

She tied the mare to the post, picked up the notebook and pen, fished out the business card, wiped down her sweaty palms and entered the phone booth.

"Hello, I'm trying to reach Christopher Morris," she said after dialing.

"Speaking." The voice sounded gruff and efficient.

"Mr. Morris, this is Eliza Struder. We've met once or twice at the farmers market here in Grand Creek, and you expressed an interest in wholesaling my Amish dolls."

After a short pause, Mr. Morris exclaimed, "Yes! How good to hear from you. Are you interested, then?"

"*Ja*, but my biggest concern is whether I can keep up with the increased demand…"

For twenty minutes, Eliza huddled in the booth, writing down notes as Mr. Morris explained the details of what he hoped she could do. He outlined prices, shipping dates, inventory and other bewildering concepts.

"This is a lot to take in," she finally admitted. "But I have a certain amount of motivation, since I'm sure you know I'm widowed and have a young child. My hope is to be able to support myself independently."

"I understand," Christopher replied. "And one thing to keep in mind is we can grow this from smaller beginnings. I don't wholesale to big-box stores, I wholesale to smaller mom-and-pop establishments. They understand when life gets in the way and sometime inventory is not as dependable when it's handmade as opposed to factory made. My suggestion is you take the information I've given you and mull it over, then let me know if you think you can make it work."

"*Ja*, I will do that." Eliza pressed a hand to her forehead, staring down at her scribbled notes. "Thank you, Mr. Morris."

"Will you be at the farmers market on a regular basis?"

"No, not always. But my brother and sister-in-law run the booth there, as you know, and you can always send a message through them."

"Thank you. And Ms. Struder, I certainly hope this will work out for you. I don't think I've ever seen such excellent crafts as what you make."

"*Danke!* I mean, thank you! I appreciate knowing that."

She hung up the phone and exited the booth in a thoughtful frame of mind. Christopher Morris had certainly given her a lot to think about, and the money he mentioned was generous enough to motivate her. It was possibly even generous enough to piecemeal out some of the work to another woman to expand the number of dolls she could make.

She unhitched the horse and climbed back into the buggy to do the shopping for Levy and Jane. Half an hour later, she placed her purchases in the back of the buggy and guided the horse for home.

She felt calmer. More in control. The numbers Christopher Morris quoted her would be enough to support her and Mercy if she rented a room in another town. Automatically, she guided the horse through traffic, not seeing or hearing much around her, as she mentally ran numbers and tallied a list of things she needed to do.

Things she needed to do…

Suddenly, with a powerful urge, she wanted to talk to Ruby. She needed to clear the air with Josiah's mother, to assure the older woman she, Eliza, would make everyone's life much easier by leaving the community. Feeling mature and competent, Eliza gripped the reins tighter in her hands and guided the horse toward Josiah's house. She knew he wouldn't be there—he'd be working at Levy's—so it would be an opportunity to talk to Ruby alone.

The Lapp house was built of white clapboard,

two stories tall and with a squat, comfortable look. Plain muslin curtains danced in the breeze from upstairs windows, and two large oak trees shaded the yard and porch.

Eliza tied the horse to a post near the yard. She took a deep breath, wiped the palms of her hands on her apron, climbed the porch steps and knocked.

No one answered.

Baffled, Eliza stepped back on the porch and scanned the doorway. Then she knocked again. No answer. Could Ruby be in the garden?

She skirted the house and knocked on the side kitchen door. Immediately she heard cries from inside. "Help! Help me!"

Adrenaline coursed through her. It was Ruby's voice.

The door was unlocked. Eliza burst inside. "Ruby? Ruby!"

"Over here!"

She followed the voice to the back of the house where stairs led to the second floor. Ruby lay at the bottom, panting, her face bathed in sweat.

"Ruby!" Eliza sprang to her side. "What happened?" She swallowed hard at the sight of Ruby's right foot, twisted at an unnatural angle.

"Fell down the stairs. Broke my ankle,"

panted the older woman. "Thank *Gott* you're here…"

"And thank *Gott* I've got the buggy. Come, Ruby, I'll take you to the hospital…"

Eliza crouched down and got Ruby's arm around her neck. "I'll stand up slowly," she instructed. "Brace yourself with your other arm on the stair banister. Let's get you upright first of all."

Ruby sucked in her breath and closed her eyes. Eliza eased upward while Ruby gripped the newel post and pulled. After a few agonizing moments, she was upright.

"How am I going to get you to the buggy?" muttered Eliza. It would entail getting Ruby out of the house, down the porch steps, across the yard, and into the buggy seat. She thought about racing home and getting Josiah, but didn't want to leave Ruby alone or take the time to chase after him.

"Maybe I can hop…" Ruby wheezed.

"No. That will jar you too much. I'll carry you," she decided. "On my back."

"Can you?"

"*Ja*, sure. You can't weigh all that much." Eliza turned so her back faced Ruby, then crouched down. "It's the only way."

"This impinges on my dignity," groused Ruby. She put her arms around Eliza's neck.

"Well, if you can still joke around, you'll live," retorted Eliza. "Hang on tight now." She slowly straightened up. She felt a quiver of pain run through Ruby's body, but the older woman said nothing as Eliza made her way outside and toward the buggy with the patient horse.

Getting Ruby into the buggy took some maneuvering, as well as grunts of pain, but at last she was settled into the seat. Eliza untied the horse, climbed into the buggy and started the animal at a brisk trot toward the town's small hospital.

"Thank you," murmured Ruby at last.

"Don't mention it." Eliza concentrated on directing the horse as swiftly as possible.

"No, I have to mention it." Ruby bit her lip and kept her eyes on the passing scenery. "I haven't treated you well since you returned to the community, and now you're doing me this kindness."

"Well, it's not like I could leave you there on the floor with a broken ankle." Eliza spoke with some asperity. "How long were you there?"

"At least an hour."

Eliza winced. "It must have been agonizing. It's just pure dumb luck I happened along when I did."

"No, not luck. *Gott* sent you."

Eliza glanced over. Ruby's mouth was drawn

with pain, but her chin was up in a defiant gesture.

"Maybe," Eliza acknowledged, then added, "Don't try to talk, Ruby. I know you must be in extreme pain right now."

"It doesn't feel good," the other woman admitted. "*Ja, Gott* sent you."

Eliza hardly knew what to say, so she concentrated on guiding the horse rapidly through town.

"Why did you come to the house?" asked Ruby. "Were you coming to see Josiah?"

"No, I knew he would be at work. I came to see you," admitted Eliza. She paused at a stop sign, then guided the horse to the left, urging him to a trot. "I—I wanted to talk to you."

"About what?"

"Now isn't the time to get into it. I'll explain later. There's the hospital."

She drew the horse up to the portico of the emergency entrance. "Stay here, I'll get some help," she ordered. She handed Ruby the reins, hopped down from the buggy and dashed inside.

"I have an older woman in the buggy with a broken ankle," she told the receptionist breathlessly.

The emergency room was otherwise deserted, so within moments a swarm of burly aides had

Ruby lifted out of the buggy and into a wheel-chair, then she was whisked away into the bowels of the hospital.

Eliza guided the horse to a shaded hitching post reserved for the town's Amish population. She wished someone in the community had a telephone so she could call and tell them where she was. But for the moment, there was nothing she could do but stay put and pray for Ruby's recovery.

She sat in the waiting room, while a silent TV flickered in one corner. She leafed through magazines depicting fashion and makeup that didn't concern or interest her. After a while she tossed a magazine aside and sank into contemplation.

Was it, as Ruby implied, *Gott* who had sent her to Josiah's house just as Ruby needed help? Certainly she was not in the habit of visiting that home. Why today?

Because she was going to talk to Ruby about her business, and assure the older woman her financial independence meant she could leave the community and start fresh somewhere else. This meant she would no longer be tempted by Josiah.

But why that sudden and powerful urge to talk to Ruby—was that *Gott* directing her to the older woman's aid?

Maybe.

An hour ticked by, then ninety minutes. At last, the double doors to the interior of the hospital opened and a white-coated physician emerged. "Miss Struder?"

"Ja?" Eliza bobbed to her feet.

"I'm Dr. Kocinski. I understand you brought Mrs. Lapp here." He held out a hand to shake.

"Ja," she replied, returning the gesture. "I found her injured in her house. What bone broke? Will she be able to walk soon?"

"She broke a part of the ankle called the talus. It was a clean fracture, and we put her in a temporary walking cast. We've also scanned her ankle for a custom-made 3D-printed cast, which will be far more comfortable for her. It will be ready in about three days. I've prescribed her some pain medication, as well."

Eliza blew out a breath. "Thank you. I don't think I've ever been as scared as when I found her, alone in the house, at the bottom of the stairs."

"I'm grateful you *did* find her. She said she was there for about an hour before you came along." The doctor rubbed his chin and smiled. "She said she misjudged you before, but now she thinks the world of you. I assume you know what that means."

"She said that?" Struck dumb for a moment, she stared at the doctor.

Before she could gather her thoughts, the double doors opened again and a nurse wheeled Ruby into the waiting room. Her right foot and ankle were encased in plaster, and she held a pair of crutches on her lap.

Eliza darted over and crouched before the woman. "How are you feeling?"

"Better," said Ruby. The strain of fear and pain was gone from her face. "But a lot of that could be attributed to the medicine they have me on."

"Whatever works." Eliza blew out a breath, then grinned. "I've been so worried."

The older woman smiled back, the first genuine smile of friendliness Eliza could remember. "I'll be fine, thanks to you."

"Are you ready to go home?"

"*Ja*, I can imagine Josiah is worried sick. But first, I want to take a detour. I'll tell you about it in the buggy."

Eliza raised her eyebrows but didn't press. Instead, she asked the doctor, "How can we get her into the buggy?"

"If you'll drive it under the portico, we have aides who can lift her in."

"*Ja, gut.* Ruby, I'll be right back."

She trotted outside and unhitched the horse, then guided the buggy under the portico. Two strong aides flanked Ruby's wheelchair. Within a few moments, she was safely ensconced in the buggy.

"Three days," warned the doctor. "That's when your new cast will be ready, and you'll like it much better than this one. You have your appointment card?"

"*Ja*. Thank you for everything," Ruby told him.

Eliza clucked to the horse, and the buggy started for home.

"What kind of detour do you want to make?" asked Eliza, as she stopped at an intersection.

"Before I answer, I want to know why you came by the house. You said you came by to talk to me?"

"*Ja*." Eliza kept her eyes on the horse's ears. "I came to tell you about a conversation I had with the *Englisch* wholesaler who wants to represent my dolls. He will buy as many as I can make. In fact, I don't know if I can make enough to keep up with what he wants, but that's a different issue. The point is, I now have a business that—if I'm careful—can support me and Mercy. So… So… So I've decided to leave Grand Creek."

"Leave!" Ruby jerked upright, then winced in pain. "Leave where?"

"I don't know. But I thought it would make everyone's life easier if I left the community."

"Everyone's life easier? Or mine?"

Eliza glanced over and saw warmth in Ruby's eyes. "Yours," she admitted. "You know there's an interest between your son and myself. You've also made it clear you don't welcome that interest. I have too much baggage around my feet. Perhaps it would be better if I left."

"Oh, Eliza…" Ruby sniffed. "Then it's more important than ever that you take me on this detour. I—I want to go talk to the bishop."

"The bishop?" Eliza was so startled, she forgot to pass the buggy through the green light, and had to wait until the light changed again. "Why do you want to talk to the bishop?"

"Because I have a great sin to confess."

"Sin? What sin?"

"The way I've sinned against you." Ruby's words were quiet and dignified.

Eliza gaped. "Ruby, how strong is that pain medication you're on?"

Ruby gave her a ghost of a smile. "I had a lot of time to think when I was lying on the floor, before you found me. Maybe *Gott* was talking to me. But I realized I misjudged you for a reason you couldn't know. It's time you know the truth, and I want the bishop to hear, as well. So *ja*, please take me to the bishop's house."

Eliza directed the horse toward the back of the farmhouse where the bishop and his wife lived, then hopped out of the buggy to hitch the animal to a post. Then she assisted Ruby out of the buggy.

"This might not be a good idea," Eliza said as she braced the woman so she wouldn't have to bear weight on her foot. "Maybe I should ask the bishop to come out here?"

"*Danke*, but I'll be fine." Her lips tightened as her good foot touched ground and she adjusted the crutches Eliza now handed to her.

"Go slow," Eliza ordered the older woman. "You don't want to overdo your leg so soon after having it set."

"While I'm on these pain medications, it feels fine. Well, mostly." Ruby let Eliza guide her. "Let's go. I want to get this over with." There was a tremor of nervousness in her voice.

Eliza drew near and knocked on the door.

The bishop's wife opened and regarded the visitors with astonishment. *"Guder nammidaag."*

"Guder nammidaag," replied Eliza. "Is Bishop Kemp home? It's important."

"Ja, he's in back." The woman's eyes darted back and forth between Eliza and Ruby. "Come in."

Eliza, slowing her steps to accommodate

Ruby, entered the living room. In a few moments, the bishop appeared. "*Guder nammidaag*, Eliza. And… Ruby? What's this all about?"

"Bishop Kemp, I came to confess a great sin…" began Ruby.

"Your leg—what happened?" asked the bishop.

"It's a long story. Perhaps we can sit down?"

"*Ja.*" He gestured toward the living room while his wife tactfully withdrew.

Ruby sank into a rocking chair with a sigh while Eliza perched in a nearby seat. The bishop settled into a large chair and waited.

"First of all, my leg." Ruby gestured toward her cast. "I fell down the stairs this afternoon and broke my ankle. Josiah doesn't even know I had an accident. Eliza found me and took me to the hospital. But I spent about an hour on the floor, helpless to move, before she came. During that hour, I had a lot of time to think even though I was in pain. And what I thought about was why I was feeling so hostile toward Eliza, and about the possibility of a courtship between her and my son. Then, what do you know, it was Eliza who found me and brought me to the hospital. Was that not *Gott*'s doing?"

The bishop gave a wary nod, and Eliza found herself holding her breath waiting for what would come next.

Ruby clasped and unclasped her hands. "I asked Eliza to bring me here this afternoon before she took me home because I need to explain why I felt and behaved the way I did. *Gott* tells us to confess our sins, so I'm here to confess."

"Ruby, if you've just had your ankle set, is this the time?" said the bishop. "I'm sure you must be in pain…"

Ruby waved a hand. "No. The time is now."

The bishop nodded and subsided.

"To explain," Ruby told him, "I have to go back a long time, long before you became the bishop. The fact that you don't know about my past means the gossip never reached you, for which I'm grateful. Bishop, the reason for my hostility toward Eliza is because I saw myself in her. I, too, left the community during my *rumspringa* and lived some wild times in the *Englisch* world." She glanced at Eliza. "But unlike you, I wasn't married when I had my first baby."

Chapter Sixteen

Eliza's jaw dropped. She gaped at the older woman, thunderstruck.

Ruby nodded. "The parallels between us are eerie. I couldn't take care of my newborn son on my own, either. I was alone in the outside world, with no family and no church connections. But unlike you, I gave him up for adoption to an *Englischer* family. I came home ashamed and humiliated. My parents knew what happened, but they kept it a secret. And my husband knew. All my life, the weight of giving up my baby has been on me. I have confidence the family who raised him loved him very much, but giving him up tore a hole in my heart." Tears welled up and spilled over her cheeks. "When I looked at you, all I could see was me at your age. I—I wanted to save my last-born son from getting tangled up with the same kind of problems I had to overcome with my firstborn son."

Bishop Kemp was silent through this confession. Finally he spoke, and his voice was gentle. "And why are you telling us this today, Ruby?"

"Because *Gott* directed me to." Ruby fished a handkerchief out of her pocket and mopped her eyes. "After I fell, I started wondering if *Gott* had sent me a broken ankle to force me to examine my conscience, to understand why I objected to Eliza's return and Josiah's interest in her."

Eliza remembered what Catherine had once told her about people with scandalous pasts. *There are more of us around than you think*, Catherine had said. *A fair number of us older women have done something we're ashamed of. I'm not going to name names, of course, but I want you to remember that. A number of us older women have done something we're ashamed of... I want you to remember what I'm saying, because something tells me it may be useful to you someday.*

So obviously Catherine knew of Ruby's secret, but wisely kept it to herself.

Ruby sniffed and pleated the handkerchief in her lap. "I realized—or perhaps *Gott* told me— that Eliza wasn't the bogeyman I made her out to be. Instead, I was the one at fault. I—I don't think I ever forgave myself for what I did—not for giving up my son, because that was the best thing to do, but in getting pregnant with him in the first place." She gave Eliza a tearful look. "It was easier to blame you than to forgive myself. I thought I was doing the best thing by discouraging Josiah from becoming entangled with a woman with similar baggage. But you were married. I w-wasn't." She broke down and sobbed in earnest.

Her heart full, Eliza knelt beside Ruby and put her arms around the older woman. Ruby leaned into her and cried. After a few minutes, the storm passed. Ruby withdrew and buried her face in her handkerchief.

"Ruby." Eliza looked up at her and kept her voice low. "Your husband knew of your past, but he loved you deeply anyway. Do you not think Josiah is capable of the same thing and can overlook the past I've had?"

"Ja." Ruby mopped her eyes and lifted her head. "And that's another thing I realized. *Gott* gave me a wonderful and loving marriage, despite my *youngie* rebellion. When I came back to the community, I wanted nothing more than to be baptized. But… But I've been against *you* getting baptized. That was evil of me, and I ask forgiveness."

Bishop Kemp was shaking his head and smiling at the same time. "Ruby, you're a remarkable woman. There is no reason for you to confess this, but you did. I can assure you, at least on my part, I will never reveal to anyone else what you said in this room. And Eliza…" He turned. "Something nudges at me. Ruby said you found her after she fell down the stairs. How did you find her? Why did you go to her house?"

Momentarily stunned to be in the hot seat, it was Eliza's turn to clasp and unclasp her hands. She stood and went back to her chair. "I—I went to talk to her about a decision I made. I have a sewing business now, with a wholesaler interested in buying what I make. It would be enough to support Mercy and me if we left to go elsewhere."

The bishop's bushy eyebrows shot up into his thinning hairline. "Leave! Why would you leave?"

"Because I thought it would be easier on everyone if I took my baggage elsewhere." She kept her voice low.

"She means me," blurted Ruby. "This is why I wanted to confess my past. Eliza, I don't want you to leave."

"Things have changed now, for sure and certain," admitted Eliza. She didn't dare give in to the wild hope that flared inside her.

"There's an element missing here, though,"

said Bishop Kemp. "And that's Josiah. He should be involved in these decisions. Eliza, can you go find him? It would give me a chance to talk to Ruby in private."

"*Ja. Ja*, sure." Feeling on the verge of babbling, Eliza stood up. "I'm sure he's working on the house expansion. Or maybe he's already home. I'll find him." She turned and fled.

Outside, next to the patient horse, she put a hand on his neck and closed her eyes. She was so unnerved that prayers almost wouldn't come. Almost. She breathed a request for calmness. Then she unhitched the horse, swung into the seat of the buggy and started for home.

"Wow, that took a long time," commented Jane, standing outside next to the barn with Levy as Eliza returned. "How did the phone call go with the wholesaler?"

"Fine, but I'll tell you about it later. I've had a *verrückt* afternoon. The reason I'm so late is Ruby broke her ankle and I had to take her to the hospital." Over the distressed exclamations of her brother and sister-in-law, Eliza held up a hand. "I'm just grateful I had the buggy. It's a long story but I can't get into it now. I need to find Josiah. Levy, is he still here?"

"No, he went home." Levy gestured toward the horse. "Do you still want the buggy? It would be quicker."

"No, let the poor horse rest. He's been very patient all afternoon. I'll run." She jerked her head toward Jane. "Can you still watch Mercy?"

"*Ja*, sure. She's napping right now anyway. You just go find Josiah." She flapped a hand.

"*Danke.*" Eliza picked up her skirts and ran, glad for the excuse to burn off some of the energy coursing through her, her thoughts a jumble as she raced through the summer countryside.

Panting, she drew up to Josiah's house. She found him in the barn, just finishing up the milking.

"Eliza!" He gaped at her. "Are you okay?"

"Josiah, it's your mother. There wasn't time to leave a note. She broke her ankle…"

He paled as she described the incidents of the afternoon. "But she's okay," she concluded. "Right now she's at the bishop's house."

"The bishop's? Why?"

"I—I think it's best if she does the explaining." Eliza knew Josiah had no idea he had an unknown older half-brother out in the world. It wasn't her place to tell him. "Please, just come with me. The bishop asked me to find you."

To his credit, he didn't dither. He snapped lids on the buckets of fresh milk and moved them to a dark corner of the barn. He dusted off some of the sawdust left over from the afternoon's labor, then nodded. "Let's go."

As she trotted beside him toward the bishop's house, she breathlessly explained how she'd found Ruby and brought her to the hospital to have her ankle set. He didn't ask why she happened to be at his house at that moment, and she didn't explain.

Eliza knocked at the bishop's door and was called to enter. She and Josiah stepped inside. The bishop sat in the same chair where Eliza had left him. Ruby, her face swollen and tearstained, actually looked more at peace.

"Mamm!" Josiah darted toward his mother and dropped to one knee in front of her. "Eliza told me what happened. How are you feeling?" He touched the cast encasing her ankle.

"Sore," admitted Ruby. "But I'm on pain medicine right now. Josiah, *lieb*, we didn't ask you here to fuss over my ankle. Has Eliza explained anything about the conversation I had with the bishop?"

"What conversation?" He looked bewildered.

"It wasn't my story to tell," explained Eliza.

The older woman nodded. "Yet another testament to your character, child. Josiah, sit down. There's a lot to explain."

Ruby spoke for nearly half an hour, and during that time Josiah hardly said a word. He felt shocked, startled and grave in turn.

At the end of Ruby's story, a short silence fell on the room. "So I have another brother somewhere," he stated.

"Half-brother," Ruby corrected. "It was a closed adoption. I don't know anything about him—where he is, what they named him. It's a chapter that's finished, and one I will ask you to keep to yourself. You're not a gossiper, Josiah. Neither is Eliza. I can trust you two to keep my secret."

"Ja," said Eliza. "No one knows better the importance of starting over. I will never hold your past against you, Ruby."

The older woman nodded. "I understand now how good and caring a woman you are, Eliza. You just temporarily lost your way when you left us. But the path back can be found. I'm a living testament to that."

"If you're referring to baptism, I think I agree with you. Bishop—" Eliza turned to the church leader "—my doubts are gone. I would like to be considered for baptism."

Josiah felt a wild flare of hope. For Eliza to be certain of her desire for baptism... For his mother to make a complete about-face in her attitude toward Eliza...

A smile lit the bishop's face. "Welcome back, child," he said. "I've prayed that was the course you'd take. But first, I must ask something of you."

Eliza's eyes widened at the request. "Yes?" she said warily.

"To forgive me for misjudging you. It seems you were right, and gossips turned innocent actions into something else."

"Of course, Bishop," Eliza practically whispered. "I forgive you. And Ruby…" She turned to face the older woman. "If I may ask, what do you plan to do now?"

"What do you mean?" His mother looked confused.

"I mean, I have a proposal to make, a business arrangement, but I don't know if you'd be interested. Even more, I don't know if you'd be interested because it would mean working with me."

"What kind of proposal?" inquired the bishop.

Eliza turned toward the church leader. "I don't know if you've heard this story, so let me repeat it now. I'm sure Ruby hasn't heard it." She took a deep breath. "When I was still out in the *Englisch* world, just before I came back to the community, I was at my wit's end. My husband was dead, my baby was gone, my faith was far away. I was lower than I ever thought possible. One day I crept into an *Englischer* church when it was deserted. I wept and prayed.

The pastor found me, and when he learned my story, he and his wife paid for my return trip here. They wouldn't hear of me paying them back, and simply asked for me to pay the favor forward someday."

"*Ja*, I've heard that story…" began the bishop.

Eliza turned. "Ruby, *Gott* led me to the notion that my debt should be repaid…to *you*. As I said before, I have the opportunity to grow my doll-making business much larger and work through a wholesaler. But I can't do it alone. I need a partner, one with excellent sewing skills. Are you interested?"

Josiah's mouth dropped open. In that moment, he felt a surge of love and respect for this young woman who had been through so much and had stayed true to her faith in the face of strong headwinds.

He glanced around and saw the others were equally dumbfounded. His mother was the first to break the silence. She snapped her mouth shut and Josiah saw fresh tears in her eyes. "Why would you want *me*?" she choked. "I'm the one who's done you wrong in so many ways."

"I asked the same question of the *Englisch* pastor and his wife," replied Eliza gently. "I asked why they would help someone like me, the lowest of the low, who had messed up her life so badly. I don't think I need to remind you it's how *Gott* works."

Bishop Kemp spoke up. "Does she have to give you an answer right away?"

"*Nein*, of course not. Not at all. But I've been anxious to repay the debt laid upon me, and this is the answer I believe *Gott* suggested to me a few days ago. Not necessarily to form a partnership, but at least to make the offer. It's—it's my way of saying I forgive you," she added to Ruby.

"Then I suggest," interjected the bishop, "that Ruby not give you an answer right now. Emotions are too high at the moment, and business arrangements are secondary to sorting out the truth of the matter. Ruby, my son can drive you home in our buggy. I'd like to speak with Josiah and Eliza alone."

After Ruby's departure, Josiah looked a bit stunned. Bishop Kemp regarded him with a touch of amusement. "This all comes as surprise to you?" he inquired.

"*Ja.*" Josiah passed a hand over his face. "A complete surprise. I had no idea *Mamm* had a baby out of wedlock."

"Now, Josiah…" The bishop adopted a sterner expression. "Your mother told me she's the one who started the rumors about you and Eliza meeting in secret. May I ask if there was any truth behind the rumors?"

"No." Josiah's confusion vanished, and he met the bishop's eyes with confidence. "Eliza has behaved with perfect decorum. If anyone could be accused of improper behavior, the blame would fall on me. I asked her to marry me once, and she refused because she didn't want her reputation to tarnish my own."

"Well, Eliza, I owe you an apology," were the bishop's unexpected words.

Eliza flushed. "Actually, I was going to offer you one of my own. I shouldn't have lost my temper with you last week."

"Just as I shouldn't have lent my ear toward gossip. Now." The bishop leaned back in his chair. "With Ruby remorseful for her part in causing conflict, how is it between you two?"

Eliza clasped her hands and didn't dare glance at Josiah.

But Josiah didn't hesitate. "Bishop, I've been in love with Eliza since before she left the community years ago. I tried to put aside those feelings after she returned, especially in light of my mother's hostility. I tried courting other women, more as a balm to my ego than anything else, but from the moment Eliza returned, I knew she was the one for me."

"And you, Eliza?" The bishop turned toward her, and she saw a subdued twinkle in his eyes.

She bit her lip and sat very still. "I think Josiah summed it up very well," she offered. "I made it clear I wouldn't be the cause of conflict between him and his mother. But if that's no longer an issue…" Her voice trembled.

"Then we may be having a wedding in November," summarized the bishop with a smile. Then he turned. "Josiah, Eliza has a child. If you marry her, will you raise the child as your own?"

"*Ja!* Of course!" Josiah looked startled. "That's not even in question. I will be happy to become Mercy's father."

"Then I think my job is finished here." With a chuckle, the bishop rose to his feet. "I'm sure you two have a lot to talk about, and my wife is holding supper for me."

Thus dismissed, Eliza stumbled to her feet and staggered out the door, suddenly weak in the knees and filled with a powerful need to ponder all that had happened. She felt stunned. She made it to the gate around the bishop's yard and leaned over it, gulping for air.

"Eliza?" Josiah came up behind her and put a hand on her back.

She whirled around and caught him in a hard embrace, too overcome to speak.

For long moments she clung to him, feeling the pressure of his arms wrapped around her back and knowing those arms would soon belong to her forever.

At last he drew back, but Josiah kept his arms locked in the small of her back. She saw moisture in his eyes. "I never thought I'd be free to court you," he whispered, touching his forehead to hers.

She gave a shaky laugh. "What a difference a few hours makes. *Gott ist gut.*"

"*Ja.* He is." With some reluctance, but aware they were outdoors and in view of anyone who cared to look, he released her. "Do you think Mercy would like having a baby brother or sister soon?"

This time Eliza didn't told back. Her laugh pealed out and echoed against the nearby buildings.

Epilogue

The brisk November weather was, Eliza felt, a gift from *Gott* for the wedding. Women bustled around the room, preparing food—getting turkeys and chickens ready for roasting, cracking nuts, setting up tables.

Eliza put Mercy down and let her toddle throughout the room. The child was steady on her feet now, and inclined to get in the way as people bustled around. Ruby was supervising the preparations for the wedding that would take place in two days. Normally the ceremony would be at the bride's house, but with Jane only a few weeks away from having her first baby, Ruby offered to host it instead.

"Penny for your thoughts?" Josiah came to stand beside her.

"Just counting my blessings." She smiled at the man to whom she would be irrevocably joined within forty-eight hours. "I'm so grateful to *Gott* for what He had planned for me. I can't remember now why I didn't think I was worthy to be baptized, yet now I am. Your *mamm* has been a blessing. Jane and Levy have been blessings. And now Mercy will have a father."

Josiah bent to pick up Mercy as she wandered nearby. "Isn't that so, *liebling*?" He nuzzled the baby's face and Mercy giggled. "*Ach, ja*, you're right. *Gott* has blessed us more than I ever thought."

"And Ruby is doing better making dolls than I am now. She's the one who figured out how to speed up the process. Between us, we're making as many as the wholesaler can handle."

"I think this business has given her a new purpose in life." Josiah's eyes twinkled. "She's been full of chatter about building it up even more. She's even talked about roping her sister, my aunt, into it. My aunt is an excellent seamstress."

"Her sister?" Eliza wrinkled her forehead, remembering. "Doesn't she live in Montana now?"

"*Ja*, she just moved there with a new branch church that opened up last year. *Mamm* has always had a hankering to see the West, so she may go visit."

"But I thought she liked the *daadi haus* you built her in back!"

"She does. She loves it. Have you seen her little kitchen? She's already furnished it. A visit to Montana would be just that, a visit. Besides, she wants to be close to Mercy. Being a *graemmaemm* comes naturally to her."

"It's nice to have a mother again." Eliza sighed with contentment. "I haven't had one since I was twelve. Ruby has stepped into that role for me. What a change in her attitude from a year ago."

"Not just hers, but yours, too."

"What do you mean?"

"I mean, you've finally forgiven yourself for your past," replied Josiah. "For a long time, you labored under a feeling of inferiority, ain't so? But redemption is all *Gott* wants. He forgave you a long time ago. The only thing left was for you to forgive yourself, and it seems you have."

"I think you're right." She gazed at Josiah in wonder. "I never stopped to think about it, but you're right."

He leaned in to give her a swift and verboten kiss.

Eliza blushed and drew back. "Josiah… People are around."

"But soon they won't be." He grinned. "Soon I'll have you all to myself."

Eliza smiled. "I can't wait."

* * * * *

If you enjoyed this book by Patrice Lewis, be sure to pick up

The Amish Newcomer
Amish Baby Lessons

Available now from Love Inspired!

Find more great reads at www.LoveInspired.com

Dear Reader,

I hope you enjoyed Eliza's story of redemption. She illustrates a concept dear to my heart—namely, it's almost never too late to turn one's life around.

I do a fair bit of writing on how to live a simpler life, and I realized simple living can be boiled down to just three words: *Make good choices*.

Think about it. Eliza regretted the choices she made in her past, and was determined to make better choices in the future. That option is open to all of us. We may not live an Amish lifestyle, but we can all live a simpler life by our choices.

I love hearing from readers and welcome emails at patricelewis1305@mail.com.

Patrice

Get 4 FREE REWARDS!

We'll send you 2 FREE Books plus 2 FREE Mystery Gifts.

Love Inspired books feature uplifting stories where faith helps guide you through life's challenges and discover the promise of a new beginning.

FREE
Value Over
$20

YES! Please send me 2 FREE Love Inspired Romance novels and my 2 FREE mystery gifts (gifts are worth about $10 retail). After receiving them, if I don't wish to receive any more books, I can return the shipping statement marked "cancel." If I don't cancel, I will receive 6 brand-new novels every month and be billed just $5.24 each for the regular-print edition or $5.99 each for the larger-print edition in the U.S., or $5.74 each for the regular-print edition or $6.24 each for the larger-print edition in Canada. That's a savings of at least 13% off the cover price. It's quite a bargain! Shipping and handling is just 50¢ per book in the U.S. and $1.25 per book in Canada.* I understand that accepting the 2 free books and gifts places me under no obligation to buy anything. I can always return a shipment and cancel at any time. The free books and gifts are mine to keep no matter what I decide.

Choose one: ☐ **Love Inspired Romance Regular-Print** (105/305 IDN GNWC) ☐ **Love Inspired Romance Larger-Print** (122/322 IDN GNWC)

Name (please print)

Address   Apt. #

City   State/Province   Zip/Postal Code

Email: Please check this box ☐ if you would like to receive newsletters and promotional emails from Harlequin Enterprises ULC and its affiliates. You can unsubscribe anytime.

> Mail to the **Harlequin Reader Service:**
> **IN U.S.A.:** P.O. Box 1341, Buffalo, NY 14240-8531
> **IN CANADA:** P.O. Box 603, Fort Erie, Ontario L2A 5X3

Want to try 2 free books from another series? Call 1-800-873-8635 or visit www.ReaderService.com.

*Terms and prices subject to change without notice. Prices do not include sales taxes, which will be charged (if applicable) based on your state or country of residence. Canadian residents will be charged applicable taxes. Offer not valid in Quebec. This offer is limited to one order per household. Books received may not be as shown. Not valid for current subscribers to Love Inspired Romance books. All orders subject to approval. Credit or debit balances in a customer's account(s) may be offset by any other outstanding balance owed by or to the customer. Please allow 4 to 6 weeks for delivery. Offer available while quantities last.

Your Privacy—Your information is being collected by Harlequin Enterprises ULC, operating as Harlequin Reader Service. For a complete summary of the information we collect, how we use this information and to whom it is disclosed, please visit our privacy notice located at corporate.harlequin.com/privacy-notice. From time to time we may also exchange your personal information with reputable third parties. If you wish to opt out of this sharing of your personal information, please visit readerservice.com/consumerschoice or call 1-800-873-8635. **Notice to California Residents**—Under California law, you have specific rights to control and access your data. For more information on these rights and how to exercise them, visit corporate.harlequin.com/california-privacy.

LIR2IR

HARLEQUIN SELECTS COLLECTION

19 FREE BOOKS IN ALL!

From Robyn Carr to RaeAnne Thayne to Linda Lael Miller and Sherryl Woods we promise (actually, GUARANTEE!) each author in the Harlequin Selects collection has seen their name on the *New York Times* or *USA TODAY* bestseller lists!